D0595028

Hannah caught her breath. Pieces of bone and hand-painted pottery were all through the loose dirt, both in the soil thrown up by the woodchuck, and in the fresh earth dug out by Hunter. Hannah noticed uncomfortably that these old bones did not look like the animal bones she sometimes found in Hunter's home under the back porch.

"Hey, Walt!" Mell screeched, thinking the same thing.

"He's running Papa's chain saw. He can't hear you," Hannah protested.

"I'll go get him, then." Mell raced off, leaping over logs and piles of brush before Hannah could stop her. "Hey," she yelled, "we found bones—real people bones. Somebody's dead here in the woods!"

Other books in the
Hannah's
Island
S E R I E S

About the Author

Eric E. Wiggin was born on a farm in Albion, Maine in 1939. As a former Maine pastor, Yankee school–teacher, news reporter, and editor of a Maine–published Christian tabloid, Wiggin is intimately familiar with the Pine Tree State and her people. He has strived to model Hannah and Walt after courageous examples of the Maine Christian youth he knows well.

Wiggin's ancestors include Hannah Bradstreet Wiggin, and one of his four granddaughters is Hannah Snyder. But his greatest model for the *Hannah's Island* series is Hannah, mother of the Prophet Samuel, known for her faith and courage in adversity.

Wiggin's twelve novels for youth and adults are set in rural or small-town Maine. The woods, fields, and pasture lanes of the Wiggin family farm sloping toward a vast Waldo County bog furnish a natural tapestry for the setting of many of his books.

Author Wiggin now lives in rural Fruitport, Michigan with his wife, Dorothy, and their youngest son, Bradstreet.

The Lesson of the Ancient Bones

Eric Wiggin

Emerald Books

P.O. Box 635
Lynnwood, WA 98046

The Lesson of the Ancient Bones
Copyright © 1996
Eric E. Wiggin

All Rights Reserved.

ISBN 1-883002-27-3

Published by Emerald Books
P.O. Box 635
Lynnwood, Washington 98046

Printed in the United States of America.

Contents

Chapter One

Old Bones of Warriors

"What do boys know about dogs, anyway?" Melanie Sampson wrinkled her nose, frowning at Hannah.

Hannah did not answer Mell's angry remark at once. Instead, she chuckled as she tied her big black horse's bridle to the white trunk of a paper birch left by the loggers. Hannah remembered how she had once tried to give Hunter the hound to Walt. A dog is a boy's animal, she had tried to make herself believe then. That was before Mell and her family had come to live on Beaver Island in Moosehead Lake, Maine.

Hannah now watched her big brother, Walt. His muscles rippled as he worked steadily with a chain saw, cutting treetops into firewood to heat Beaver Lodge. Farther on, the two French Canadien loggers Papa had hired were busy felling trees for lumber. Papa was paying Walt ten dollars a load for all the firewood he could salvage out of leftover limbs and tops from the crew's logging.

"Walt and Hunter get along just fine," Hannah

7

laughed, patting her horse's sleek coat. "Besides, he's right. The men can't have my dog chasing rabbits and woodchucks all around their work. Someone might get hurt."

"You mentioned woodchucks—isn't that a chuck hole Hunter's digging into?" Mell pointed to where Hannah's long-legged, tri-colored hound was digging furiously into a gravel ridge, which Papa called a 'horseback.'

"Sure looks like a woodchuck hole to me. Too big for a rabbit. Let's go see." Hannah swung up into her Western saddle, then waited as Mell climbed a stump to scramble onto Ebony behind her.

"What have you found there, silly?" Hannah looked down from the saddle moments later as Hunter, whining and frustrated, whimpered at the entrance to a groundhog burrow in the ridge. "Smart woodchuck!" Hannah laughed. "You'll have to catch that fellow in the open if you really want to eat him." Only inches into the earth, the woodchuck's hole squeezed between a big rock and a large, tough root. Hunter was unable to dig any farther.

Suddenly, Mell shouted. "Hey, look! What is that? An old flower pot?" She slid off Ebony's back and seized onto a large clay urn lying half-hidden in a clump of raspberry bushes.

She lifted it high so Hannah could see the painted designs that covered it. Since the pot had only old dirt dried on it, Hannah decided that the woodchuck, not Hunter, had dug it out of the gravel ridge, probably months ago.

"Oh, yuck! It's full of ol' bones." Mell turned the pot upside down, and pieces of bone and old teeth fell out. Curious, she kicked the dirt with her sneaker. A piece of broken pottery popped out. "Broken dishes—they're all over!"

Hannah jumped down from Ebony. "You're right," she said, pushing past a bush loaded with green, unripe berries. Hannah caught her breath. Pieces of bone and hand-painted pottery were all through the loose dirt, both in the soil thrown up by the woodchuck, and in the fresh earth dug out by Hunter. Hannah noticed uncomfortably that these old bones did not look like the animal bones she sometimes found in Hunter's home under the back porch.

"Hey, Walt!" Mell screeched, thinking the same thing.

"He's running Papa's chain saw. He can't hear you," Hannah protested.

"I'll go get him, then." Mell raced off, leaping over logs and piles of brush before Hannah could stop her. "Hey," she yelled, "we found bones—real people bones. Somebody's dead here in the woods, an' parts of their body were stuffed in a jar!"

Walt and the loggers put down their tools and followed Mell to the woodchuck burrow.

"This is a very strange tooth, *non?*" Pierre Pellitier, Uncle Joe's French Canadien cousin, and his partner, Jacques LaFonde, had done work for Papa before.

"Is it human?" Hannah worried.

Walt examined the tooth and small piece of jaw bone. "It looks human all right. And it's old."

"It's a real people tooth," Mell yelled. "We've found a dead body. Gotta call the cops!"

"Not so fast," chuckled Mr. Pellitier. "The enamel on this tooth is ground down, like whoever this creature was did a lot of gnawing on hard stuff. Chewing roots, *non?*"

"*Non,* I mean *oui*—yes," Walt said, agreeing with Uncle Joe's cousin. "Maybe a farm animal. A hundred

years ago, this whole island was the Sampson farm."
Walt glanced at Melanie, whose great-grandfather
once owned the island.

"So...so I guess maybe this ridge was an old
dump—sorta like a landfill," Hannah concluded.

"Just the same," Walt said, "we ought to check
things out. May I borrow that jar?"

"Yeah." Mell passed Walt the jar, and he began
to scoop up bits of bone and teeth.

"Show this stuff to Papa, okay?" Walt told Hannah.
"We need to be sure."

"I think," said Jacques LaFonde, "ze jar, she is
Indian, old Abnaki, mebbe."

"*Oui,*" agreed Pierre. "Years ago many farm people bought Indian jars and baskets for storage. There
were no cardboard boxes then."

※ ※ ※ ※ ※ ※ ※

"Is it human, Papa?" Hannah peered at the bits
of old bone Papa had stuck together with super
glue. He was working under his high-intensity
lamp. She watched as he carefully rolled the bowl-
shaped bone fragment over, then began to fit the
teeth in place with a pair of tweezers.

"Yes," Papa said. "See here." He pointed to where
the skull had begun to take shape. "Even though we
have just a small portion of it, you can see it's going
to be much too large for an animal skull."

Hannah sighed. "Then Melanie's right. We ought
to call the police."

"No rush. If this was a murder, it happened
many years ago. A few more days won't make much
difference."

"Maybe Hunter and that woodchuck dug up an
old cemetery," suggested Walt, who had just come

in from the barn where he'd been milking Molly.
"Didn't a lot of these old farms have their own
graveyards?"

"Don't be silly, Walt. There weren't any grave-
stones! I've been over every inch of this island with
Ebony and Hunter since we moved here. There are
no cemeteries on Beaver Island."

"Hannah's right, Walt," Papa agreed. He pointed
to the county map that hung on the wall of his
small office in Beaver Lodge. "Every graveyard in
Piscataquis County is on that map. There are no
graveyards on Beaver Island."

"Then it comes back to murder. Why else would
someone bury a body with its head stuck in a jar?"
Walt demanded an answer right now.

Papa smiled softly and leaned back in his swivel
chair. "I remember a line from a poem: 'Old bones of
warriors underground.' Tell you what. I have to drive
to Bangor in a couple of days on business. There's
an archaeologist at the University of Maine, near
there. He studies old bones from early cultures, and
he might be interested in looking at this stuff. Think
Mell will part with that jar for a few days?"

"Mell's as attached to that jar as Hunter is to an
old soup bone," Hannah worried. "But she might let
it go to the university if she could go with us on the
trip. I'll look out for her."

"I guess Mama could spare you for a day—both
of you." Papa nodded to Walt. "It's a good chance for
the two of you to get a head start on your history
lessons for when you home school next fall."

Chapter Two

Dogs Don't Make a Difference

"Down, boy! Sit," Hannah commanded as Hunter strained at his leash and whimpered at the fancy French poodle. "She'd never look at you. You're just a mutt from the woods."

But the poodle turned, wagging her tail and running toward Hunter until she reached the end of her own leash. The excited poodle nearly upset the middle-aged gentleman walking her.

The man wore a tweed coat and a felt hat, though it was a summer day, and Hannah thought he looked rather dignified.

"Easy, Susie. That's a good girl," the gentleman said firmly, but warmly. "Lie still, girl."

Susie the poodle obeyed at once, folding her legs beneath her curly white coat. She hunkered down with her head on her paws.

"You can let your English foxhound come closer, now," the man chuckled. "I think they'd like to make friends." He set his briefcase on the carefully clipped grass of the university's tree-lined common. "What is your foxhound's name?"

"Hunter," said Hannah. "And he's not a fancy English foxhound. Plain ol' mongrel—Lab and basset," she modestly added.

"Well, well," the friendly gentleman laughed, watching Hunter and Susie sniff each other and nuzzle their wet noses together. "He's 100 percent dog, like my Susie. Dogs don't make a difference, whether they're mongrel or pedigreed. Did you ever notice that?"

"I...I guess I hadn't noticed," Hannah stammered, not quite sure what the man meant.

"He means race or looks don't mean nothin' t' dogs, just so the other dog's friendly," Mell guessed.

"You're a very perceptive young lady," the man said.

"P'ceptive? Does that mean I'm smart?" Mell cocked her head to one side.

"Well..."

"Anyways, I'm only average smart. We're here to meet the smartest man in Maine, Dr. Hans Frankenmuth, the archaeologist. He's gonna tell us what these ol' bones are in this here crockery jar." Mell unwrapped the old jar from the sweater she had used to protect it.

"Well, I..." The man looked so startled that Hannah thought he would faint. "That's pre-Columbian I believe—a treasure. Where on earth did you get it?"

"Found it. A woodchuck rooted it out of a gravel bank on Beaver Island. It was under some raspberry bushes." Mell's eyes shined merrily at the stranger's sudden interest in her prize. "Raspberries ain't ripe yet, though," she added as a matter of fact.

"Raspberries!" The man found it funny that Mell thought the berries were as important as the old jar.

"Perhaps we'd better..." said Hannah. She shot a warning glance at Mell. The stranger's attention was making her uncomfortable, even if he was friendly. Hunter, she noticed, suffered no such discomfort. He lay quietly on the grass as Susie the poodle snuggled her curly head into his neck.

"No, no!" said the man, looking worried. He seemed positively startled when Mell carelessly tucked the jar under one arm like she would an old doll. "I was on my way to my office just now to meet Mr. Harry Parmenter, who's bringing me some Indian artifacts to examine," he added.

"I'm Mr. Parmenter," said Papa, who stepped up just then with Walt. "The girls got ahead of us while we were locking some things in the trunk of our car." He nodded toward the parking lot at the end of the university's grassy common.

"Well, it *is* good to see you and your fine family!" The gentleman extended his hand to Papa. "I'm Professor Frankenmuth, the archaeologist."

"How about that!" Papa chuckled, shaking the professor's hand. "I thought I might have a bit of trouble finding you, but I guess Hannah and Mell found you first."

"Won't you come up to my office," the professor invited warmly, motioning toward a big old stone building at the end of the common. "It's upstairs above the library."

Hannah suddenly wanted very much to visit this interesting man in his office, but she knew she had to stay outside with Hunter. But maybe since the professor had a dog... She shot a worried glance at Papa.

"Hunter is certainly welcome," Doctor Frankenmuth said, seeing Hannah's worry. "We can take the elevator upstairs. My Susie sleeps in a box behind my desk, and since they seem to have made friends, I'm sure he'll lie quietly while we talk."

"This is the genuine article!" The professor held Mell's old crockery jar up to the window as he peered at it with a magnifying glass. "You say you found it in a gravel bank?"

Melanie was grinning as if she'd just discovered a buried chest of gold. "Yes, sir. Right where a wood-chuck dug it out."

Hannah said nothing. She could not believe that an old jar dug out of the woods on Beaver Island could be important. So she sat in the corner of Professor Frankenmuth's office, quietly scratching Hunter's ears as he rested next to Susie the poodle's box.

"How can you tell it's not a fake?" Papa asked. "I've seen jars just like it for sale at the Northwoods Trading Post in Laketon."

"Yeah—and there's Aunt Theresa's flower pot," Hannah blurted out suddenly. Papa had a point. Did this strange professor merely *want* to believe the old vase was valuable?

Doctor Frankenmuth looked at Hannah, frowning. Hannah blushed.

"Like yourself, I've seen lots of reproductions," he said to Hannah and Papa. "The tourists buy them, thinking they're genuine Indian pottery. Most of them were made in Taiwan. But see here—the shape is irregular. *Early* Indians made all their pottery by hand without a potter's wheel. All *modern* clay pots are spun on a wheel, which makes them symmetrical, or evenly shaped."

"But I *saw* an Indian using a potter's wheel. He

was making vases at the museum in the state library." Hannah was indignant now.

"True, true," the professor said patiently. "The potter's wheel was invented at least 3,000 years ago. It's mentioned in the Bible, in the Book of Jeremiah." The professor rested his hand on a well-worn Bible that lay on his desk. "Some of my colleagues chuckle a bit at my trust in this old book, but it's my main guide, in archaeology *and* my daily life."

"Oh!" Hannah cried suddenly. It startled her that this educated man was a Christian. She was also reminded of something she'd learned in her history book. She had seen a picture of an Indian family dragging its burden on two poles pulled by a dog. "Indians didn't use wheels at all," she said aloud. "So even though people used potter's wheels in Bible times, Indians didn't have potter's wheels, I guess."

The professor held up a finger. "Precisely. But they did use the potter's wheel after it was brought here from Europe. So the display you saw at the state library was correct for more recent Native Americans. This vase is pre-Columbian."

"Very old, then," Papa said.

"Do...do you mean it was made before Columbus came to America?" Now Hannah was excited.

"On October 12, 1492—I learned that in school last year," put in Mell. "That must have been a long time ago."

"But for a jar to remain buried in the earth all those years...?" Papa still could not believe it.

"You said a gravel bank?" The professor looked at Mell.

"Well, yeah. It's not regular dirt."

"It's a horseback," Walt explained. "Solid gravel, clear across our island. We have a gravel pit in one place, where Papa and I sometimes dig out gravel to fix our road."

"Ah, yes," the professor sighed. "Some of those gravel horsebacks are full of old artifacts. They furnished a dry place where Abnakis could bury their dead. Gravel is well drained, so artifacts don't decay very fast."

Using large tweezers, he picked up a piece of the bone the girls had found in the old jar. "I'll need to run some tests on this to learn its age. May I keep it for a few days, along with the jar?"

"I...I guess so," said Hannah.

"I want my jar back soon's you figger out how old it is," Mell insisted.

Chapter Three

Abnaki Island

Moments after their visit with Doctor Frankenmuth, Hannah held Hunter's leash as Papa made a phone call from the library lobby, downstairs.

"You can't bring that dog into the library," growled a security guard, who stepped up while Papa used the pay phone.

"He's been visiting upstairs with Professor Frankenmuth's poodle, Susie, and we're on our way out." Hannah smiled brightly.

"Hannah's ol' houn' just discovered a 'portant pre-Columbian Indian artifact," Mell told the guard, proud of the scientific facts she'd just learned. "He's got good manners," she added quickly.

The guard shot a peevish glance at Papa, who was deep in a phone conversation, then strode off.

"Well," said Papa, sounding worried as he hung up the phone, "the man I needed to see in Bangor this morning had an emergency. He won't be in for several hours. While we wait, how'd you kids like to visit an Indian village where pottery like Hunter found is still made?"

"Wow!" shouted Mell.

"Right near here?" Walt wondered.

"Sure is," chuckled Papa. "Ever hear of Abnaki Island?"

"You mean the Penobscot reservation?" asked Hannah, who had read her Maine history. "The Penobscots were part of the Abnaki tribe that once inhabited all of Maine and parts of Eastern Canada."

"This river," explained Papa, "was one of the two disputed boundaries between the French settlers of old Acadia and the English settlers of New England. During the French and Indian Wars, the Abnaki nation fought on the side of the French, and the Iroquois fought for the English." Papa pointed toward the black, broad expanse of the Penobscot River as they rolled along the highway.

"But I learned in my history book that the Kennebec River was the disputed boundary of the French and English," Hannah said, puzzled. "The Kennebec is the river that runs south from Moosehead Lake, where we live."

"Papa said 'disputed' boundary," Walt put in thoughtfully. Both rivers were disputed as boundaries.

"The land between the rivers was claimed by both the French and English," Papa told them. "So when the English built settlements—farms and villages—between these two great rivers, Abnaki Indian parties went downriver against them."

Papa turned the car onto a bridge that led to an island in the Penobscot River, above the city of Bangor.

"Where are the tepees?" asked Mell.

"Indians don't live in tepees anymore," Walt said, as they drove into the village.

"Actually, Eastern Abnaki Indians, such as the folks living on Abnaki Island, never did use tepees like the Plains Indians of the West. They had no buffalo skins to make them of. They used bark wigwams and lodges in the old days, though some wigwams were shaped like tepees," Papa explained.

Hannah was quiet as they drove through the reservation. It was a cluster of mostly white, older houses, much like the village of Laketon, near her own Beaver Island home. The lawns were neatly trimmed, and modern cars and pickup trucks sat in the driveways. Several round-faced children riding bikes smiled as Papa and the kids rolled past.

"Arf!" said Hunter, his head sticking out the window. He was always ready to make friends.

Papa parked the car near the bridge from the mainland, and Hannah, Mell, Walt, and Hunter followed him to the outdoor store offering Native American goods.

"This is all genuine handmade pottery," said the smiling Abnaki woman, who ran the open stand.

"I can see that," Papa chuckled. He set the vase down after looking at the bottom. "Who made it?"

"We make it right here. My son is an art student at the University of Maine. He supports himself by creating exact copies of old Indian pottery. He makes Abnaki patterns from all over Maine— Norridgewock, Passamaquoddy, and Micmac—as well as Penobscot designs."

"Can we watch him make some?" Mell asked excitedly.

"Be glad to show you," the lady answered. "He can come, too," she added, pointing to Hunter, when she saw Hannah's disappointed look. "Beautiful hound. Just hang onto him."

"Hunter found an old Indian vase in the woods on Beaver Island," Hannah said, grinning.

"Might be one of ours. Campers buy them for storage, then leave them all over, like an old can or bottle."

Hannah was about to explain to the lady that the pot was very old and had bones in it. But Papa looked at her sternly. He did not wish to be bothered by crowds of curious people.

A young man with straight black hair sat at a potter's wheel in a room behind the open shop. He wore a beaded headband to keep his hair back, and his feet, dressed in moosehide moccasins, were busy kicking a large stone wheel to keep the flat potter's wheel spinning. He was carefully shaping a large vase on the slowly turning wheel, and his wet hands were covered with gooey, gray clay.

"This is Bear-of-the-Woods," said his mother.

"Don't...don't potter's wheels use electric motors?" Hannah asked, surprised that this one was foot-powered. "The one I saw in Augusta did."

Bear-of-the-Woods looked up. "Sure they do— usually," he agreed, chuckling. "But this design is thousands of years old. 'Behold, he wrought a work on the wheels.' My friends call me Ben," Bear added.

"'Behold, he wrought...' That's from the Book of Jeremiah, in the Bible," Hannah said, remembering Professor Frankenmuth.

"Two thousand six hundred years ago," said Walt, who had studied Bible history.

"Wow. That's before Columbus discovered America!" cried Mell.

Ben Bear-of-the-Woods grinned wryly. "A few

years before. Actually, I built this potter's wheel myself. I copied it from a picture in my Bible encyclopedia. It's very much like the one Prophet Jeremiah saw long, long ago."

"But why did you make it, instead of just buying a modern electric wheel?" asked Walt.

"I get asked that a lot," Ben said. "I figure that since the pottery I make isn't really old, the best I can do is use an old-style wheel." He gave the stone wheel a kick and the flat wheel began to spin again. "It's even got a wobble, see." He held his hand next to the spinning soft clay vase to show the wobble. "This means that every vase or jar I make is slightly out of round, like the old-time stuff my ancestors shaped without a wheel, before Columbus."

"Pre-Columbian." Mell remembered the professor's words.

"Where do you get your clay?" asked Papa, noticing it was gray, not red like Western Indian pottery.

"Along the banks of the Penobscot River, just upstream from here. Abnakis have made pottery from gray Penobscot River clay for thousands of years."

"Are...are you a Christian?" Walt asked, getting bold. He was curious after hearing the young potter quote the Bible.

"Sure am," Ben said, smiling. "A lot of Penobscots, Micmacs, and other Indians are following the old religions, though. Some of them are puzzled, angry even, when they see me making old-time pottery but not following their traditional, non-Christian religion."

"You can certainly be a Christian and still practice much of your Abnaki culture," Papa agreed. "I guess many folks find that hard to understand."

"Hi, Chief!" Ben greeted a dignified gentleman

who stepped into the workroom just then wearing sharply creased slacks and a tweed jacket.

"Hey, Ben! How are y' doin'?" chuckled the visitor. The man grinned, showing a pleasant row of white teeth in a round, tanned face. Instead of a tie, the fellow wore a heavy string of rough, handmade beads. Hannah noticed, too, that the man's straight gray hair was braided into a long pigtail that hung down his back.

Ben Bear-of-the-Woods turned to Papa. "This is Chief LeRoi Littledeer," Ben said, with a polite nod toward the smiling stranger. "The chief is the head shaman among the Abnaki tribes all across Maine and Eastern Canada."

"My pleasure to meet you, sir," said Papa. "I'm Harry Parmenter," he added, remembering that Ben didn't know his name. "These are my children, Walt and Hannah, and their friend, Mell."

"A fine family. I have granddaughters about your ages." Chief Littledeer winked at Mell, who grinned shyly.

"Well, if I'm going to make that meeting back in Bangor, we have to go," Papa said. Hannah heard Mr. Littledeer talking in earnest with Ben as they walked toward their car.

Papa took the expressway around the factories and new houses as they drove back toward the city of Bangor. Hannah let herself be amazed at how, in mere minutes, they had left an Indian culture on an island in the Penobscot River and re-entered the fast-moving city.

"Papa, what's a shaman?" she asked at last.

"I...I really don't know," Papa admitted.

"I think a shaman is a religious leader, what we sometimes call a medicine man," Walt said.

"Then he'd be an Indian doctor," Mell put in.

"Well, yes and no," Papa said, thinking. "In some cultures the healer and the religious leader are different people."

"So, why did Ben call Mr. Littledeer 'Chief'?" Hannah wondered.

"Because," said Walt, who seemed to have all the answers this morning, "in Native American culture 'chief' doesn't just mean a political leader. It's also a title of respect for any tribal leader."

Hannah figured that what Walt said made sense. But there was still so much about Abnaki culture she didn't understand. Hannah made up her mind to get out her book on Native American culture and figure some of these things out when she got home to Beaver Island.

Chapter Four

Let's Make Pies

"Hannah, what are you making?"

Smiling, Hannah put down her rolling pin and turned to face the inquisitive girl sitting on Mama's kitchen stool. Mell Sampson hugged the wooden stool with her skinny legs, her curious eyes wide with wonder. Her skinned knees and bruised shins reminded Hannah of herself when she was not quite nine.

"I'm making pies," Hannah laughed. "You helped me make those pumpkin pies for Thanksgiving, remember?"

"Looks like cookies t' me," Melanie said, wrinkling her pug nose. "My gramma made cookies once, when we lived in New Hampshire."

"I...I guess your mom doesn't bake cookies, or pies either?" Hannah asked gently. She did not wish to sound rude. Hannah already knew that moving to Beaver Island from the large city of Manchester, New Hampshire had been a shock to Mell's family.

"Naw. My mom doesn't cook cookies," Mell

affirmed. "But you said that was a pie," she added, puzzled. "Where's the punkin batter?"

"It's gonna be a pie, all right, but not pumpkin. I'm rolling out the crust now." Hannah flipped the pastry dough over, then flopped it into a ten-inch glass pie plate. "See!" She spun the plate lightly on her fingertips so Mell could watch as she deftly trimmed the extra dough with a table knife.

Mama stepped into the kitchen just then. She held her breath, watching silently as Hannah risked breaking one of Beaver Lodge's best pie plates while showing Mell how good she was at trimming crust.

"When you have your own pie plates you may hold them on your fingertips," Mama said sternly, after Hannah set down the pie plate. "With mine, keep them firmly on the counter while trimming the pastry."

"Yes, Mama." Hannah felt sheepish at being caught playing tricks with the dishes. Mama had not told her *not* to hold a pie plate on the fingertips, exactly. But Hannah knew it was one of those things about which Mama would say, "You ought to know better."

"We all love your pies, though." Mama bent over and kissed Hannah's cheek. "How many are you making?"

"Four—apple-rhubarb."

"Your pies won't last long in a house full of hungry tourists," Mama worried. "And we only have six quarts of canned apples left from last fall."

"That's why I'm adding lots of rhubarb. It'll be weeks before we have enough fresh fruit raised here on Beaver Island for pies." Hannah pointed to a mixing bowl full of sugared ruby red rhubarb, which she'd sliced just before rolling the crust. "That's going into the pies," she said, as much to Mell as to Mama.

"My mom's *never* made a pie. We get ours at the store," Mell said sadly. "Can I help, like at Thanksgiving?"

"Sure," Hannah agreed. But she had the task nearly done. It did not seem fair for Mell to help only with the dishes.

Mama knew what Hannah was thinking. "You'll need more rhubarb if you're making all ten-inch pies."

"I can get it!" Mell yelled. "It's in the barnyard!" Mell loved to help herself to the Parmenters' rhubarb and munch a tart stalk while walking home.

"You'll need this." Hannah handed Mell an old paring knife, and the younger girl raced off into the sunshine, her sneakers flying. The screen door banged behind her.

"I do believe you've got yourself a helper," Mama chuckled.

"Ha-an-na-a-ah! E-e-e-e-e-k!!"

Hannah cocked her head and listened to the distant, muffled yells. It had been several minutes since Melanie left for the rhubarb patch behind Papa's barn. Hannah had begun to wonder if her helper had wandered off to play. Perhaps a couple of Sam Sampson's fancy potbellied pigs had got loose again and Mell was chasing them home.

"Hannah!!" came another shriek.

Hannah stepped outside, wearing a long, white baker's apron over her jeans. No sign of Mell. Then she heard her. From behind the barn came screams, sobs, and threats.

By the time Hannah reached the barnyard fence, Mell had Bullet, Molly's bull calf, backing away.

Though Bullet was a teenager in calf years, he was really only months old. Papa had kept the young bull out of the open pasture since the morning he and Hunter had had a fight. Bullet had nearly killed Hannah's hound. He could be dangerous, Hannah knew.

She scrambled over the wire fence instead of using the gate, to get between Melanie and Bullet quicker. Walt must have let Bullet into the barnyard while he cleaned the frisky animal's stall, not knowing Mell was out there cutting rhubarb. Hannah could see that Mell had met Bullet as she rounded the barn with an armload of fresh rhubarb stalks. Bullet's head was probably down to eat grass, his stubby horns lowered. He couldn't have imagined in his tiny, bullheaded brain that a little girl would be afraid of him.

"That wild bull is gonna charge at me an' poke holes in me with his horns," wailed Mell. "He'll hook me t' death!" Then gritting her teeth, Mell cried, "I'll stab you with this knife if you get any closer, nasty ol' bull!"

"Shoo, silly beast," Hannah yelled. She shook her apron at Bullet, the flour flying about and filling the air.

Bullet turned, tearing across the muddy barnyard. He bounded over the fence, barreled up the hillside, then with another flying leap, cleared the pasture fence where his mother, Molly, and Hannah's horse, Ebony, munched the tender grass.

"I'll murder that mean mad bull if he gets near me with those horns again." Mell brandished the short paring knife in the air to show how she planned to do Bullet in.

"He's only a calf," Hannah said, hugging Mell. "He was more scared than you were. Now I think we have another job for that knife," she added, noticing that the rhubarb Mell had cut was trampled into the barnyard mud.

By the time Mell chopped up all the rhubarb, she had filled another large mixing bowl.

"Oh, my!" Hannah exclaimed. She could see that they now had enough fruit for *five* pies. "Now we have too much rhubarb."

"Can't we just make 'nother pie, Han? Remember all those punkin ones we made?"

Hannah liked Mell to call her 'Han.' It was a friendly name, like she was a loving big sister. "I guess we *could* make another one," she laughed, eyeing the half-quart of leftover apples and the fist-sized ball of pastry dough she was about to put in the refrigerator. "Would your mom like you to bring home a fresh pie?" Hannah was already reaching for another pie plate.

"Mom loves pies," Mell said, her eyes shining in delight. "I can make it myself."

"Well..." Hannah passed Melanie the rolling pin, remembering that she had taught her how to roll dough at Thanksgiving. Then Hannah bent down to pop the finished pies into the oven of the big, restaurant-size gas stove Papa had installed in Beaver Lodge's kitchen. "Just you wait a minute."

By the time Hannah straightened up, Mell had begun to roll out the dough. At least she was trying to.

"Ec-c-ch-h!" Mell frowned at the sticky mess stuck all over her rolling pin.

Hannah bit her lip. She could not let herself scold Mell for not waiting. She sometimes had to learn by making mistakes, too, she realized. And cleaning up your own messes helps teach you to be patient with others.

"Let me help you," Hannah murmured gently, showing Mell how to dust the dough with flour to keep it from sticking.

In no time at all Mell was rolling the pastry without any sticking to the pin. She got the bottom crust a bit too thick, and she had to roll the top crust extra thin to make it cover. *Never mind,* thought Hannah. *It's Mell's own pie!*

"My mom's gonna be proud of me," Mell chirped nearly an hour later, when five piping hot pies came from the oven.

Chapter Five

Unexpected Visitors

"Indians! We've got Indians! Come see!"

Hannah was baby-sitting Paul Sampson for the day while his parents were gone to the mainland. She was used to Paul's screams and yells, so she didn't always run at once when he hollered. Still, since Paul had once nearly died after throwing a rock at a hornet's nest, Hannah knew better than to wait too long.

But what was this about Indians?

An eight-man canoe was coming toward Beaver Lodge's dock when Hannah stepped onto the porch. Though it was still early, she thought at first that it might be from the children's camp far down the lake, where kids were sometimes dressed as Native American Abnakis and taught to paddle long canoes.

But these were adults—mostly tan, muscular young men, several without shirts. In the rear sat a stately, middle-aged man in shorts. He wore a plaid shirt and suspenders, and his face was partly hidden by a floppy straw hat.

A man sitting in the middle also wore a broad-brimmed straw hat, as well as sunglasses for protection from the sun. From his hat an eagle feather poked out—at least it looked to Hannah like an eagle feather, the special feather used to adorn an Indian chief. Like the older man in shorts, the fellow held his jeans up with suspenders. And a gray pigtail fell down his back from beneath his hat. He seemed to be a guest of the rest, though, for he sat in the canoe with his arms folded as all the others paddled.

In the front seat of the canoe sat the only woman. She seemed young, and her braided black hair was held back by an Indian-style sweatband beaded with wampum. She wore a single turkey feather tucked into one braid. Though her eyes were hidden by sunglasses, her smile showed the prettiest, whitest row of teeth Hannah had ever seen.

The beautiful girl tossed a rope over a post as the canoe pulled up. Then the guys helped hitch the canoe to Papa's dock. The older man in the rear climbed out first.

"Up you go, Chief," chuckled one of the young fellows, cupping his hands under the man's foot to boost him.

Hannah noticed that the man was pale-skinned, and had knobby knees. She almost giggled out loud when the others called him 'Chief.' Hannah thought he looked more like he should be called 'Paleface.' If the others were Native Americans, he surely was not.

The man in the floppy straw hat walked directly toward Beaver Lodge, while the others rested on the dock. Hannah noticed that although the young men were tanned, several had light hair. Somebody is playing Indian, she decided. Still, these were not children, so it puzzled her to see them playing this way.

The "chief" carried a cane, though he didn't seem to need it to walk. Instead, he swung it or tucked it under his arm. *Where have I seen him before?* Hannah pondered, beginning to recognize the man. She tried to focus her memory on a dignified gentleman wearing a tweed coat and carrying a cane—a gentleman leading a poodle, Susie, that had made friends with Hunter.

"Oh!" Hannah squealed. "Professor..."

"...Frankenmuth, the archaeologist. And you're Hannah," he chuckled.

"I...I don't understand."

The professor-chief smiled broadly. "Is Mr. Parmenter home, please? All will be apparent soon."

In her excitement over seeing Doctor Frankenmuth again, Hannah forgot the other gentleman for several moments. When she finally did look back, she saw that he stood holding his backpack, apart from the young men as if he did not belong with them. And as with Professor Frankenmuth, Hannah knew she'd seen the man somewhere.

But where?

Papa did not seem surprised at Doctor Frankenmuth's sudden arrival at Beaver Lodge. "Come in," he said, noticing the professor mopping his sweaty face with a big, red bandanna. "It's air-conditioned." Papa nodded toward the folks on the dock. "Bring the rest of your crew inside, too. They look tired. It's awfully warm for so early in the day."

Hannah looked at Papa with a question on her face.

"Oh," said Papa. "Doctor Frankenmuth phoned the other day while you were on the mainland. I don't know how we forgot to tell you."

"But what *ever* is going on?" Hannah insisted.

"This is the professor's class of summer archae-ology students from the University of Maine," Papa explained, grinning. "I've given them permission to conduct a dig in the gravel ridge where you and Mell and Hunter found the bones and old vase."

"Excuse me, Hannah," Papa said suddenly. He stepped away to greet the gentleman with the gray pigtail, who now followed the young men and one young woman up Beaver Lodge's porch steps.

"Chief Littledeer, it's good to see you again!" Hannah heard Papa say. "Glad you could come along."

"Usually one chief is enough for so small a tribe," Chief Littledeer laughed. He gave a knowing nod toward Professor Frankenmuth.

The professor only grinned, as if they held a pri-vate joke between them. Then he turned back to Hannah.

"What's a dig?" Hannah asked. She knew a woodchuck had been digging there.

"A dig is a scientific process," the professor explained. "We carefully uncover old artifacts, layer by layer. Sometimes we screen the gravel to find stuff we'd miss by just digging."

Screen the gravel. Hannah knew what that meant. She'd helped Walt screen gravel by tossing it through coarse screen to get the rocks out. Papa had then used the sand that fell through the screen for mortar when he and Sam built a new fireplace for Beaver Lodge.

"Well," Hannah volunteered, "maybe I can help."

"We're counting on you as our chauffeur," said the professor. "We're going home each evening, of course, but we're buying meals here at the lodge. Once in a while we'll need rides across the island."

"Chauffeur?" Hannah was not sure what he meant by that.

"I told Doctor Frankenmuth that you and Walt could take turns driving the students across the island," Papa explained, turning from his conversation with Chief Littledeer. "They'll park their canoe over there. But you'll need to bring them here for meals."

"Except when we eat picnic lunches—that'll be most days, of course," said the professor, very satisfied with the arrangements indeed. "We won't be much bother."

Hannah shot a surprised glance at Walt's old Chevy truck. He had bolted several seats in place—the seats Uncle Joe had used when the truck was an excursion bus on the ice-covered lake. Hannah had thought Walt was getting his truck ready to give Mama and Papa's hotel guests a ride.

"But I..." Hannah wanted very much to drive the college students back and forth on the logging road. She had learned to drive Papa's John Deere tractor, and Papa had let her take it across the island alone a couple times. She had driven Walt's truck several times, too.

"It's all right, Hannah," Mama said, stepping onto the porch. "I can watch Paul for a little while while you're gone."

※　※　※　※　※　※　※

"Hi. I'm Lucille LaVerdiere," said the young woman with the black braids as she hopped onto the front seat next to Hannah. "Call me Lucy."

"Hi, Lucy. I'm Hannah." Hannah started the truck motor. She really wanted to be friendly, but she decided to keep her mind on her driving.

"Have you been living on Beaver Island long?" Lucy's words were clipped, and when she said 'been' it sounded like 'bean.'

"About three years." Hannah glanced at the Indian girl. At least she *looked* Indian. But she had an accent that made her sound like the Queen of England, whom Hannah had once heard on Aunt Theresa's TV making a speech. Perhaps Lucy was only pretending to be Indian.

Either way, her smile was so bright that Hannah *had* to be friendly, even if she needed to pay attention to her driving.

"Are...are you English?" Hannah asked, embarrassed.

"My ancestors had already been here in North America for more than 3,000 years when Captain John Smith met Pocahontas," laughed Lucy. "I'm Indian—Native North American. Micmac. That's an Abnaki tribe, related to the Maine Penobscots. Chief Littledeer's Micmac, too." Lucy pointed over her shoulder with her thumb.

"But your accent? You...you sound English."

"When the Pilgrims landed, they met an Indian who spoke English with a British accent," Lucy teased mysteriously.

"Who are you, really?" Hannah was no longer nervous. Lucy was going to be fun—maybe like a big sister, she decided at once.

Hannah stopped the truck and got out to open the gate through the old stone wall. When she got back, Lucy had her foot on the brake pedal.

"You forgot to set the hand brake," Lucy said softly so the others would not hear.

"Thanks." Hannah's ears burned red. Her passengers might have gone rolling and bouncing across the pasture and through the fence.

"You were asking about me," Lucy said, as they drove beneath the pines and hemlocks lining the woods road. "I have a French name, Indian blood, and I sound English or British. But I guess we're all a mixture, aren't we?"

"Yes, I guess we are," Hannah said thoughtfully. She remembered what Professor Frankenmuth had said: "Dogs don't make a difference." There was something in the Bible about people not making a difference either. Hannah guessed she'd better look it up when she got home.

Lucy flashed Hannah another smile. "Actually, I'm a Canadian, from the province of Prince Edward Island. Chief Littledeer is also a Canadian, from the province of New Brunswick."

Pierre Pellitier and Jacques LaFonde were the only Canadians Hannah knew. Papa had explained one day that Mr. Pellitier and Mr. LaFonde were *Canadiens*, which means French Canadians from the province of Quebec. Their accent was French. Even Uncle Joe Boudreau, who had always lived in Maine, sounded a lot like a *Canadien* to Hannah.

"Many Canadians sound English to Americans," Lucy chuckled.

"Prince Edward Island," Hannah said, thinking out loud as she tried to remember what she'd learned in geography. "That's in the Gulf of St. Lawrence, isn't it?"

"It sure is. And we call it P.E.I., or simply 'the island.'"

"Like in *Anne of the Island*," Hannah squealed. She had certainly heard of P.E.I., for she had read the famous books set in that area.

"From *Anne of Green Gables*? Yes. There's a story behind that that I may tell you sometime. I can't seem to get away from islands." They were crossing Juniper Bog Brook, and Lucy peered far down the winding stream to where it fed through a marsh, then into Moosehead Lake.

Chapter Six

In God's Eyes

"Hi, Indian!" Five-year-old Paul stared wide-eyed at the young college student with Professor Frankenmuth. Hannah had just made a trip across the island to bring the archaeology class back to Beaver Lodge for lunch. Though the student was tanned bronze and had his blond hair cut in an army butch, he wore moccasins and a beaded Indian sweatband.

The student smiled at Paul, who waited just inside the dining room door at Beaver Lodge. He had paused outside to button his shirt after reading Mama's sign: NO SHOES, NO SHIRT, NO SERVICE.

"I'm not really an Indian," the student said, "but I do like to wear moccasins."

"You look like an Indian," Paul persisted.

"Well, I suppose I do. Being outdoors a lot this spring gave me a good tan."

Paul was about to say something more when Lucy LaVerdiere came up the porch steps. "Would you like to meet a *real* Indian, Paul?" She knelt and set Paul on her bent knee. "I'll bet you'd like an Indian friend!"

"You an Indian?" Paul seemed surprised, even though it was Lucy's braids and feather that had made him think all the students in the canoe were Indians.

"Uh-huh," Lucy nodded. "I'm the only Indian in this tribe. We're here to study Native American culture of long ago."

"What about him?" Paul pointed at the professor.

"The Chief?" Lucy laughed. "That's just a title of respect. He's not really an Indian. The Indians call him 'Chief' 'cause he's helping them out. Did you ever hear of an Indian chief named Dr. Hans Frankenmuth?"

"I...I guess not," Paul said happily.

"So let's go wash your grubby paws so you can eat lunch with us."

"They're *hands!* Dogs have paws," Paul insisted.

"All right, hands, then. Sorry," Lucy apologized.

"Chief Littledeer, what were you doing over at the cemetery this morning?" Hannah asked politely.

Papa's new boat had just about the quietest motor on Moosehead Lake, for Papa did not like the noise of roaring motorboats. He wanted his guests to enjoy the quiet of the northern wilderness. Hannah was glad she and the shaman could talk in the boat as they buzzed toward Laketon.

It was right after lunch, and Walt had left to drive the archaeology students and their professor back to the dig in the Indian cemetery. Since Papa had to entertain hotel guests, he had asked Hannah to take Mr. Littledeer to Laketon to catch a Greyhound bus to New Brunswick, Canada.

"I needed to make peace with the spirits of the

dead." The chief smiled at Hannah, and she knew right away that he liked kids. "The spirits may be angry, otherwise."

"The spirits…" Hannah was about to disagree and tell Chief Littledeer that there are no spirits in cemeteries, since the Bible teaches that a person's spirit and soul leave when the body dies. "The spirits," Hannah began again, "why would they be angry?"

"You are a Christian, aren't you?" he asked, not answering her question directly.

"Yes."

"So is Ben Bear," he sighed. "So many of my people forsake the old ways of our ancestors."

"What are the 'old ways'? I mean, Ben Bear-of-the-Woods makes old-style Native American pottery. Isn't that an old way?" Hannah could not believe she'd been brave enough to ask Chief Littledeer to explain what he meant. She wished to tell him about Jesus, but she remembered how Jesus asked questions and dealt gently with people.

The chief sighed again. "The old religion of our fathers," he explained. "Once upon a time our people prayed to the spirits of the forest and the rivers, and had great reverence for their dead."

"I…I'm sure Ben respects his ancestors," Hannah stammered. "So does Professor Frankenmuth—at least I think they do."

"Dr. Hans Frankenmuth and I are friends," the shaman said with feeling. "He respects me as a *person* the same as I respect him as a *person*. But the professor does not respect our ancestors in the way I respect them. He can't, because like you and Ben, he does not believe as I believe.

"But because we are friends, we help each other," Mr. Littledeer added. "He is glad to share with me and my people what he and his students find in their digs. My Micmac people have learned much about our past from the work of Doctor Frankenmuth. He does much good. So I was glad to appease the spirits for him before his students dig into the graves of our ancestors."

"What does the professor believe?" Hannah asked quietly. She remembered that the professor had mentioned the Bible when they visited him at the university.

"He believes in Jesus, that He died for sins—like you believe in Jesus. The professor believes that people have no relationship with God, and can only enter into one through Jesus."

Hannah could not believe her ears. Though he wasn't a Christian, Chief Littledeer seemed to know how a person could become a Christian. He and Professor Frankenmuth must have had some good talks about spiritual things, Hannah decided.

"What do you believe, sir?" she asked quietly.

"I believe in the great spirit Manitou, who is in the water, forest, and humankind. My beliefs can never agree with your Christian beliefs."

The chief smiled and reached for his backpack as Hannah pulled the boat up to the Laketon municipal dock. "We shall meet again," he added mysteriously as he climbed onto the dock.

"See ya," Hannah cried happily.

"Take good care of my friend the professor," Mr. Littledeer laughed, waving as he strode up the street toward the bus depot.

That evening in her room Hannah read in Acts 10 about how the Lord spoke to Cornelius, an Italian officer in the Roman army, and to Peter, a

Jewish Christian. Peter was told through a vision to love Cornelius, and treat him as a brother in Christ. The Lord told Peter not to make a difference between Jews, Gentiles, Italians, Romans, or people from any place or culture. All who believe in Jesus are accepted by God into His family, Peter was told.

Hannah chuckled when she saw the silliness of trying to be prideful about one's own culture. *Most of us are mixtures, like Lucy LaVerdiere,* she thought: French name, Indian blood, Canadian citizenship, American college student—mistaken for having an English accent.

And Hannah laughed out loud when she remembered the professor's fancy pedigree poodle, Susie, nuzzling Hunter, Hannah's mutt hound, not making a difference, like Professor Frankenmuth said.

When Hannah went to sleep, she had a happy prayer in her heart. She was glad that God understood things better than she did, that He loved all the people of the world, that He loved Little Paul and all the college students, that He loved Chief Littledeer and that He loved her.

Chapter Seven

Hare Springs

Hannah sat tall in the saddle on her black stallion, Ebony, as she watched the archaeology students dig and sift. Hunter, for his part, followed his fine hound nose, circling and dashing back and forth, tracking a small animal that had passed by hours ago.

"Hi, Hannah!" Lucy LaVerdiere stepped up just then, mopping her forehead.

"What are you finding?" Hannah asked eagerly.

"A lot of human bones. No doubt this ridge was used as a cemetery by Native Americans for many years, long, long ago."

"Native Americans—Indians." Hannah rolled that over her tongue. To call these people Native Americans was not new to Hannah. But 'Indians' was the word most people used. So Hannah found it much easier simply to say 'Indians.'

"Actually, I prefer to call my ancestors by the names they called themselves: Micmac, Penobscot, or Abnaki," said Lucy. "Many of them lived and died before this land was even called America. So how

44

are we really Native *Americans?* See here." Lucy held up two objects. One was stone, and the other was rusty steel. Both had broken wooden handles sticking out of them.

"What are they?"

"They're both tomahawks. The stone one was buried much further down than the steel hatchet."

Hannah knew that Indians had got their rifles from white men. But steel tomahawks? "What does that mean?" Hannah wondered.

"It means," Lucy explained, "that Native Americans buried their dead here on Beaver Island over a period of at least several hundred years."

"Wow!" Hannah exclaimed. "But how can you be sure?"

"The stone ax head—hatchet, tomahawk, whatever—was made by Indian craftsmen long before French traders started selling them steel tools from Europe around 1540." She held it up. "The steel hatchet, which was buried much closer to the surface, may have been made as recently as 1790. We can date the steel hatchets we find by looking at their manufacturers' markings in our lab at the university."

"That's pretty impressive," Hannah agreed. "No wonder Chief Littledeer was willing to let you dig here."

"Sure. We can add a great deal to Shaman Littledeer's knowledge of his own people and culture," Lucy said.

"You had never really thought about it, had you?" Lucy laughed. "Where *did* Native Americans get steel tomahawks? They were made in Europe, in countries like Belgium and France, then brought in wooden cases across the Atlantic Ocean where they were traded to Indians for beaver furs."

"So the Indians just put handles on them," Hannah said, brightening.

"You got it! These are actually box maker's hatchets, a carpenter's tool common in Europe even today. But the stone one is much older—pre-Columbian. By comparing tools such as these, we can see how Native American cultures changed over the years."

"Professor Frankenmuth thinks our vase is pre-Columbian," Hannah said. She turned, whistling for Hunter, who came crashing through the brush after a long-legged, bouncing brown creature.

"Your hound has found himself a rabbit, looks like," Lucy chuckled.

"Sit!" Hannah commanded, as a panting Hunter trotted obediently to her side. Tongue out, Hunter rolled his languid brown eyes lovingly up at Hannah. He had learned his lesson months earlier when he ignored Hannah's command to leave off digging out a spiny porcupine.

"It's not a rabbit Hunter was chasing." Hannah's eyes were full of mischief as she told her new friend about Maine wildlife.

"A hare?"

"A snowshoe hare," Hannah said. "They have longer legs and bigger feet than cottontail rabbits."

"Bigger appetites, too!" Lucy pointed toward a circle of logs where the students ate their lunch. "They clean up the food we drop. Hey guys!" she called. "Lunch is ready!"

Hannah untied the ropes that held the feed bags in which Mama had packed sandwiches and jugs of fruit punch. She passed the bags down to Lucy.

"The hares are eating up our garden this summer," Hannah said. She watched a moment as Lucy and one of the college boys toted the food over to some stumps they were using as tables.

"Oh," said Hannah at last, when Lucy had finished helping spread out their lunch, "Mama says it's okay for you to spend the night at Beaver Lodge once in a while. You can stay up in my room."

"Mama?" Lucy raised an eyebrow, then smiled at Hannah. "The invitation is really from you, isn't it?"

"Y...yes," Hannah admitted. She had asked Mama, of course. Yet Hannah very much wanted this beautiful, friendly Micmac girl from Prince Edward Island to visit her overnight. But how does one invite a *college* girl to sleep over? Hannah remembered what Mama had said: "You just ask her."

Lucy smiled. "I'd love to."

❊　❊　❊　❊　❊　❊　❊

"Your island is a beautiful place." Lucille LaVerdiere peered across the rail of Beaver Lodge's screened porch to where the rays of the setting sun outlined Papa's barn, the hen house, and the garden plot. The garden had a new fence, and the posts cast long, eerie shadows that stretched clear across the pasture and into the forest. "Such perfect solitude," Lucy added.

"Our solitude would be more perfect if it weren't for all those rabbits," Walt grumbled. "I killed and buried eight more last night."

"Was that you I heard shooting up by the garden?" Hannah asked.

"Yeah. The rabbits dug right under our new fence."

Hannah did not correct Walt for calling Maine snowshoe hares 'rabbits.' Most folks call them that, anyway, she sighed to herself.

"This island is overrun with rab...hares," Lucy

said. "We've been watching the wildlife out by our archaeology dig. I've seen only a couple of foxes—both sick and mangy. It's a disease that kills them off."

"So now the hares have no natural enemies," said Hannah, who was learning about science and biology. "And they multiply like..."

"...Rabbits." Lucy finished Hannah's sentence, and they all laughed.

"I've got an idea," Lucy suggested after a while. "One summer on P.E.I., I learned how to trap rabbits with wire snares, set with a hairspring trigger. I'm sure that would work with snowshoe hares."

"I'd still have to kill 'em," Walt put in glumly. Clearly, he didn't like the idea.

"I don't think so. You've got some more of those old feed sacks in the barn, haven't you?"

"Sure," Walt agreed.

"Then we could trap them unharmed," Lucy pointed out. "Each afternoon, when the professor and the guys head back for the university, they could take them to the mainland and turn them loose in the woods."

"Super!" Hannah exclaimed happily.

"What are you doing, Walt?" Hannah had gone to Papa's workshop to remind her brother that it was time for family devotions. He and Lucy had disappeared into the shop right after supper, and she had returned a few minutes later without him.

"I'm fixing up some rabbit snares." Walt sat on an old stool, working with pliers and thin electric fence wire. He held up a piece of wire, in which he had made a loop in the end, then turned the wire back on itself to form a noose. There were nearly a dozen other wire snares on Papa's bench, along with a pile of forked stick triggers that Walt had whittled with his pocket knife. "Hare spring snares with hairsprings," he chuckled. "They're quick as lightning, and they don't hurt the bunnies."

"But, Walt, what pulls them up?"

"Easy. Just bend over a few chokecherry bushes along the stone wall. The rabbits hop into the wire loop to nibble the bait. They jiggle this forked stick, and bingo! The chokecherry bush straightens up with a wriggling rabbit dangling in the noose, caught but unhurt."

Two days later when Lucy left with the archaeology students to go back to the university for the night, three large sacks of squirming, whimpering snowshoe hares were loaded into the big canoe with them. The hares, thought Hannah, would surely enjoy their new home in the Maine wilderness. They would have thousands of acres of forest and fields in which to roam free.

Chapter Eight

Heart Strings

The "Laketon Express" is what Papa had jokingly started calling Walt's truck the winter before. The open-topped pickup had become Walt and Hannah's ride across the frozen lake on the days they went to Laketon Christian Academy for extra help with their home school studies.

So Hannah had not been surprised, many months ago on a Saturday morning in February, to look out the dining room window and see Walt's truck returning from Laketon on the ice. Walt, she saw, was behind the wheel—or was he? Another head, trailing a thick mane of flame red hair, was near enough Walt's shoulders to make it appear that he had become a teenage Siamese twin. Dainty gloved hands gripped the steering wheel. Several times, the red hair whipped into Walt's face. If the green eyes belonging to the redhead hadn't been watching the ruts worn across the ice in the snow, the pickup would surely have been wrecked.

"That Walt!" Hannah said to no one but herself. Though her voice was angry, she grinned as soon as the words were out of her mouth. She knew the red hair belonged to Caylin Coulson, a member of Laketon Christian Academy's squad of cheerleaders. The Coulson family had moved to Laketon from Connecticut the summer before to live in the house next door to Uncle Joe and Aunt Theresa Boudreau.

Hannah remembered how Caylin had climbed the backyard fence one day to find Walt hard at work fixing the old truck. Though several students at Laketon Christian Academy had teased Walt about driving a truck that didn't have a cab, Caylin did not laugh. As Papa once said, "Any girl worth spending time with will look at the driver, not his wheels." Hannah thought Papa was very wise.

"I'm sorry. You can't come until tomorrow night," Hannah heard Walt say.

She did not usually listen to her brother's phone chat. But he was talking to Caylin on the barn phone while she milked Molly that evening, the second week after the student archaeologists had begun their dig. Lucy LaVerdiere had climbed into the haymow to throw down a bale of hay for Bullet the bull calf, who had been tied in the barn on a stout rope since he'd scared Mell.

Months earlier, Papa made a deal with a wealthy cottage owner whose place was on a point of land just a quarter-mile from Beaver Island on the mainland. The man had had a new phone line run along the forest trail to his new log cabin. So Papa paid for a short underwater phone line that connected to the man's new line. Now Beaver Lodge had inexpensive phone service, and Papa had bought a phone extension for the barn and one for his shop, too.

"I hope I didn't spoil Walt's plans," Lucy worried, when Walt had left for the house. The nineteen-year-old came down from the haymow into the tie-up where Hannah was milking.

"You didn't spoil his plans," Hannah said softly. "When he invites Caylin to spend the night in my room, he should tell me first. I'm really sorry about this. Caylin hasn't spent the night on the island for weeks."

"I'm sure Walt checked with your parents," Lucy said, trying to smooth things over. "I can pay for my own guest room tonight."

"You're not going to pay—that's silly. And yes, Walt would never invite Caylin unless he asked Mama first. But Mama has all she can manage keeping track of the tourists, so sometimes she forgets what we've asked her. Walt and I—we've both invited too many kids to spend the night before," Hannah laughed.

"I *could* sleep in the haymow." Lucy looked into the open barn floor, where swallows darted in and out of the dying sunlight.

"All right. We'll both sleep in the haymow. I'll talk to Walt and Mama soon as we get to the lodge."

Mama understood. Hannah and Lucy could sleep in the barn, and Caylin could have Hannah's bed. "So far," Mama chuckled, "I haven't accidentally booked any tourists for the same room."

So Walt phoned Caylin. "Oh. See you Friday afternoon," he said, putting down the phone. "Caylin's decided to spend the night with Tammy Adolphsen," he told them mildly. "I've got too much to do tomorrow to entertain a girl, anyway. She'll be here late tomorrow."

※ ※ ※ ※ ※ ※ ※

Caylin Coulson eyed the young woman helping Walt load a bag of squirming snowshoe hares into the university class' canoe. Lucy was taller than Caylin—about Walt's height—and five years older. With a cheerful "See ya!" to Walt and Hannah, she took her seat in the canoe full of college students.

"Lucy, this is Caylin," Walt said as soon as Caylin finished tying her boat to the dock.

"Hi, Caylin. I've heard some good things about you." Lucy smiled, showing what Hannah thought was the prettiest row of teeth in all of Canada.

"Hi," said Caylin. She wrinkled her freckled pug nose and, without speaking to Walt, marched straight toward Beaver Lodge.

When Hannah went to her room Friday night, she found that Lucy had left half a bottle of White Shoulders perfume on her dresser. Beneath it, was a note Lucy had written on a sheet of Beaver Lodge stationery that Mama kept around for guests.

Dear Hannah,

Lucy wrote,

I enjoyed so much my stay with you. I couldn't get to town to buy a special gift, so I'm leaving you your favorite perfume.

Hannah blushed. She had teased Lucy to let her try a squirt or two of her White Shoulders every time she got it out. With both Lucy and Hannah well-sprayed with the stuff before breakfast, Papa had wisecracked that "It smells like a New York emporium in here."

P.S.,

Lucy's note continued,

Tell Walt I haven't had so much fun catching hares since I left P.E.I. You're lucky to have such a nice brother.

L.L.

Hannah left the note unfolded while she braided her hair before bed. Caylin came into the room a few moments later, after talking on the porch with Walt. She looked angry, Hannah thought. She also read Lucy's note, but she said nothing.

Saturday morning, Hannah was in the kitchen with Mama, getting breakfast for the guests. Walt was already in the barn milking Molly. Suddenly, Hannah and Mama heard a motorboat start down by Papa's dock.

They hurried to the window. Caylin, in her dad's boat, was headed for Laketon at full throttle. She had slipped silently out the back door. "It's not safe to be out there in a boat this early," Mama remarked, noticing the fog blanketing the lake.

"I know, Mama," Hannah worried. She remembered nearly crashing Papa's motorboat into the *President Lincoln II* after not heeding Mama's warning to drive slowly in the lake fog.

Sandy Parmenter waited a half-hour, then called Caylin's mom. "Yes," Hannah heard Mama say. "I understand perfectly. I remember my own feelings when I was fourteen. I phoned you mainly to be sure Caylin made it through the fog safely."

"Did I...did we do something wrong, Mama?" Hannah asked as Mama hung up the phone.

"No-oo. I believe the Lord lets things like this happen so we can take a better look at ourselves and our relationships. You and I need to pray for Walt and Caylin."

"Walt...Walt, I'm sorry," Hannah murmured, when her big brother came in with a pail of Molly's fresh milk.

"For what?" Walt snapped.

Hannah cringed, fighting back tears.

"Sis, it's not your fault," Walt said a moment

later, softening. He sighed. "I didn't mean to be rude to you. I guess Caylin needs to learn that she's not the only girl in the world."

"Do you mean...?" Hannah asked, surprised.

"No, I don't 'mean'!" Walt said. He shrugged helplessly. "You...you think of Lucy like a big sis, right?"

"Yes," Hannah answered.

"Well, I do too—mostly, anyway. That's what I mean—I think," he stammered. "Caylin will just have to get used to that, and not try to give things meanings they don't have."

Chapter Nine

Hannah's Discovery

After Sunday school at Laketon Community Church, Hannah and Walt joined a row of teens and almost-teens who sat near the front with Heather Andrews, the youth pastor's wife. Pastor Mark Andrews, who led the singing and directed the choir, would join his wife and the group of young people during the sermon.

Hannah hadn't seen Caylin Coulson during Sunday school. Aunt Theresa, who lived next door to the Coulsons, said that Mrs. Coulson was sick with the flu. So Hannah and her friends decided that Caylin had stayed home to help her mom, most likely.

Uh oh, thought Hannah, as Caylin walked in just before the start of morning worship. She walked down the center aisle of the church, then crossed the front to reach the end of the teens' pew nearest the wall. But the end seat was taken. *She can sit somewhere else. It's her choice,* Hannah thought. But then she winced at the embarrassment she was sure Caylin felt. Hannah knew it was silly, but it always made her feel stupid to cross in front of the whole church and then find no place to sit.

I'd better go sit with Mama and Papa, Hannah decided, determined not to hurt her friend who had left Beaver Island in anger only yesterday.

Hannah squirmed, then bent to reach her summer straw purse, which she'd left at her feet. Someone had carelessly kicked it out of her reach under the seat ahead. Her arm wasn't quite long enough.

"I'll get it!" The guy next to her slid down, then deftly fished her purse from beneath the seat.

"Thanks."

"Sure," he said simply.

It was Mike Wilson, the eighth grade boy who had called Hannah 'cute' at a basketball game months earlier. Hannah blushed. She glanced Walt's way, planning to tell him she was leaving to sit with their parents. But Walt had turned his back to her to pick up his Bible and Sunday school book from the seat next to him. Hannah hadn't realized there was an empty seat.

Caylin, in a yellow summer dress, was squeezing past several pairs of male knees directly toward the seat next to Walt! And she was smiling.

Hannah smiled at her friend, then quickly put her purse back beneath the seat. *Well, that's that*, she thought.

When Youth Pastor Andrews announced the opening hymn, Hannah discovered that the hymnbook rack at her knees was empty. *Rude*, she thought, seeing that Mike Wilson had grabbed the last hymnal. Hannah knew Papa had taught Walt that it's polite to let ladies go first. But Hannah realized she was thoughtlessly turning Papa's teaching around for her own selfish reasons. Besides, Mike had just been so nice about rescuing her purse from under the pew, even if it did embarrass her a little.

Now Mike offered to let Hannah share his hymn-book. Because she didn't know the words and it would have been rude to refuse, Hannah held it with Mike while she sang. *This is embarrassing,* she decided, wishing she could concentrate on her singing. *What will people think?*

By the end of the church service, Hannah had discovered a couple of things about Mike Wilson, things that frightened her a little when she thought about them on the way home. Mike had a great tenor singing voice, and he used Aqua Velva after-shave, the same brand that Papa used. *Mike's cool,* she decided. *Who cares what people think?*

All of Papa and Mama's Beaver Lodge hotel guests had left on Saturday, so Hannah, Walt, and their parents had the lodge to themselves Sunday afternoon. Hannah was propped up on a porch glider, reading *Anne of the Island,* and Walt, his long legs stretched across the rail, was working his way through next Sunday's Bible lesson. Several loons had drifted into the cove by Papa's dock, for the lake was unusually quiet. A long series of wild pip-ing sounds came from the lake as one of these handsome ringnecked waterfowl called to his mate.

Hannah looked up, her reverie with Anne Shirley disturbed. "Walt," she ventured, teasing. "Guess you got your girl back."

"Not really."

"Oh?"

"Caylin and I, we decided maybe we should spend less time together. I talked to her on the phone yesterday after she got home and cooled off.

Then I had a long talk with Mama. She helped me get some things straightened out."

"Oh?" Hannah put down her book. "Caylin took off in that motorboat in an awful hurry."

"Yeah." Walt grinned, embarrassed. "She lost her cool, alright. She can be a hothead when she thinks someone's in her territory."

"Since when is my brother her 'territory'?"

"I told her that," Walt chuckled. "I think she got the message. She apologized."

"I think she should have!" Hannah was indignant.

"We still like each other—we're friends and all that," Walt added, after a pause. "But fourteen and fifteen—that's awful young, y'know."

"I know," Hannah agreed. Even though she thought Mike Wilson was kind of neat, she knew that her first loyalty, after Jesus, was going to be to Mama and Papa for a long time to come.

"Y'know what else?"

"What?" Hannah waited to hear more. Sometimes big brothers could help you understand your own feelings about life.

"That Lucille LaVerdiere," he said, using Lucy's formal name, "she's a knockout. If I were older..." Walt's words trailed off, and he went back to his Bible study.

❊ ❊ ❊ ❊ ❊ ❊ ❊

"Papa, is it wrong for Walt to like two girls at once?" Papa was helping Hannah feed the calves in the barn that Sunday evening. Hannah had made certain that Walt was not in the barn before she spoke.

Hannah had thought of Lucy only as an older

sister. She was a little surprised to discover that Walt could like a girl who seemed to Hannah pretty much an adult.

"Do I detect a certain bit of personal interest in that question? Do you think there's something you can learn about yourself, maybe?" Papa raised a wry, bushy eyebrow, then smiled.

"Ye-es," Hannah admitted. She knew that, like her brother, she could also be confused by her feelings. Sometimes Hannah wished Papa couldn't see right through her. It made her feel like the Visible Woman, a transparent model of a human body she'd seen in a science classroom at Laketon Christian Academy.

"Mike Wilson was nice to me today. But I don't have...have any opinions about him, exactly." Hannah was fishing for words.

"And you liked it?"

"Yup."

Papa put his arm across Hannah's shoulders. "God gives us feelings long before we're ready to use these feelings or even understand them. God wants us to have enough time to learn to understand ourselves, and this takes years of growing up."

"I guess," Hannah said thoughtfully, "the Lord wants me to know Him better, first of all. That's an important way to get to know myself, too."

"'That I may know Him,'" Papa quoted from Philippians 3:10, one of Hannah's favorite Bible verses. "I think," he added carefully, "it's perfectly normal for a guy to be attracted to more than one girl, or to a girl not his own age. And your feelings when a guy is nice to you are normal, too. But it may be years before you can focus on one individual in a mature way, in a relationship called 'love.'"

Hannah hugged Papa tight, burrowing her nose

deep into his cow-smelling overalls. Right then she did not care about Aqua Velva.

"I'm glad your *my* Papa!" she said. Deep inside, Hannah had never felt happier.

Chapter Ten

The War Dance

"You must be Melanie Sampson."

Hannah eyed the young woman with the camera and cases of extra lenses with caution. "No," she said at last. "I'm Hannah Parmenter. Would you like me to take you to Mell? She lives over there." Hannah shot a finger toward a point of land jutting into Moosehead Lake. It separated Beaver Lodge from the old Sampson place. "Who are you?" she asked, smiling at the woman. The stranger had not introduced herself.

"I'm Gert Abbott, writer-photographer from the *Bangor Daily News*. Sorry. I guess you're the girl who was with Miss Sampson when she found the pre-Columbian vase."

"Actually, *he* found the vase." Hannah pointed to Hunter, whose chain was fastened to the corner of the porch.

"Who?" The news reporter seemed startled.

"Hunter, my ever-faithful houn' dog," Hannah laughed. "He stumbled over the vase while chasing a woodchuck into its hole. I'm afraid the poor chuck has been dug out of its home, with all the digging going on."

"I'm sure he has," the reporter agreed. "I stopped over there before coming here. May I shoot a few photos of you and Hunter?"

"Sure," Hannah obliged. She sat on the grass beside Hunter and let him rest his handsome head on her shoulder as the reporter circled around, snapping pictures. Moments later, the reporter was on her way to the Sampson place.

    ❋ ❋ ❋ ❋ ❋ ❋ ❋

"Hey, Hannah made the headlines!" Walt held up a copy of Friday's *Bangor Daily News*, which he had just bought in Laketon. There it was at the bottom of the front page—a photo of Hannah and Hunter. Behind them, the sign "Beaver Lodge" was in plain sight, hanging from the porch rail.

"Oh no! Not again!" Hannah remembered last time she was in the news. Not only did the *Bangor Daily News* feature her after she found the Pherson china dolls at the bottom of Moosehead Lake, but her story ran in *The Saturday Evening Post* and on "Good Morning America." The public library's doll collection was stolen after word got out about the dolls Hannah had found. A strange man had made ugly remarks to her in a restaurant. And finally, the *President Lincoln* steamboat was burned by crooks.

"Beaver Island Hound Finds Rare Indian Vase," the headline now screamed. Though there was no photo of Melanie Sampson, the article said that she was the first to spot the pre-Columbian vase, after Hunter uncovered it while crashing through raspberry bushes chasing a woodchuck. "The vase," wrote the reporter, "is believed to be thousands of years old."

"Wow!" said Hannah. "Even Professor Franken-muth admits he doesn't know how old the vase is. Why would Gert Abbott know?"

"Oh boy," groaned Papa, "the professor and his crew of college students will have no peace now. Besides, I spoke with him just last week, and he's not sure that the vase is old at all."

"Perhaps we'd better put up a 'No Trespassing' sign," suggested Mama.

"Walt," Papa said thoughtfully, "there are some plywood scraps on the rafters in my shop. I'm going to make a couple of signs, and I'll need your help."

※　※　※　※　※　※　※

"Does this mean we have to stop digging here?" Lucy asked.

Hannah held a signpost as Walt pounded it into the ground with a heavy mallet. It was several hours since the Parmenters had read the news article, and Hannah and Walt had gone in Walt's truck to the back of Beaver Island.

"No," Hannah laughed. "Papa gave you guys per-mission. We're just trying to keep the curiosity seekers from bothering you."

"*Curio* seekers, more than likely," the professor remarked. "Once the public learns we're digging, there's no end of nosy people who will come to carry off whatever free curios they like. I'm afraid one of my students made a grave mistake by calling the newspaper."

"*I* certainly did not call the newspaper," said Lucy. "I have far too much respect for my ancestors' remains to do that."

"Well, two more days next week—Monday and Tuesday—and we're out of here," Doctor Franken-muth chuckled.

"Does that mean we won't be seeing you again?" Hannah shot a worried glance at Lucy.

"Well, probably," Lucy admitted. "But I could stay overnight on the island with you next week, Hannah. Camp out, maybe?"

"I'd love it!"

* * * * * * *

"Waw-waw-waw-waw-waw-waw! Woo-woo-woo-woo!"

"Whoa, boy!" Hannah tightened Ebony's reins and brought her big black stallion to a halt.

"R-r-r-r-r-r-r!" Hunter snarled. Always ready to protect Hannah, he shot off down the logging road toward the archaeological dig.

Hannah whistled. "Come back here, feller." Not since she had discovered dozens of exotic Vietnamese potbellied pigs in the underbrush near this same forest road had Hannah been so nervous— and so afraid.

Hunter obeyed at once.

Sitting behind Hannah on Ebony, Mell dug her fingernails into Hannah's ribs. "Is it Indians?" She whispered hoarsely.

"I...I don't know." Hannah was quite sure it could not be Indians. She had already watched as Chief Littledeer danced at this cemetery. It was certainly nothing like this.

Professor Frankenmuth, Lucy, and the rest of the college students had gone back to the university for the weekend. So Hannah and Mell had decided to trot across the island this sunny Saturday afternoon to make sure everything was okay. Papa said they'd be all right, since no strange boats had stopped at the island.

"I'm not sure what it is," Hannah said, trembling.

"But *please* stop clawing me. Can't you just hug me?"

"S-sorry. Mebbe it's ghost Indians."

"Silly! There's no such things as ghosts." Still, Hannah could not forget what Mr. Littledeer had said about the spirits of the dead.

"Then w-what is it?"

"Let's find out!" Hannah said, asking the Lord for courage. "Hup, boy!"

Ebony obeyed, trotting toward the bloodcurdling hooting.

Hannah and Mell could not believe their eyes. Two teen boys were leaping around in the dig, which Professor Frankenmuth had carefully measured off with strings. Some of his strings were knocked down, and the guys were dancing and chanting like they *imagined* Apaches on the warpath did. One boy had a human skull, and he waved it above his head.

"Hey, you! Get out of there! That's a burial ground. You're trespassing on our property, besides!" Hannah's anger at the ridiculous sight completely overcame her fear. The boys were in danger of destroying several weeks' work. They had no business being on Papa's land without permission, and no business treating a cemetery this way.

The guy with the skull walked toward Hannah. "These ol' Indian bones ain't nuthin t' nobody. What're yuh gonna do about it?"

"Yeah," called the other, picking up a shirt which he'd taken off when he began to sweat during his war dance. "We were just having a little fun. We didn't hurt anything."

Hannah stared at the second fellow for a moment. It was Artie Spearrin. She hadn't seen him since Sara Melton's funeral. Sara had drowned when Artie removed the barriers on the ice at a skating party. The judge ordered him to do a hundred hours of community service for that. Hannah could not decide if she was more hurt that someone would violate a burial ground, or that Artie would participate. She thought he had changed.

Just then, Artie's pal dropped the skull. He made a grab for Ebony's bridle.

"Rrowuff! Snap!" The tide had turned before Hannah could even shout a warning. Hunter had the fellow by the arm, and the guy cried out in pain. Suddenly, the boy pulled a knife from a sheath on his belt.

"HUNTER!" screamed Hannah.

Hunter let go and dodged the knife.

"Dave! Let's scram!" Artie yelled.

Clutching a bleeding arm, the fake warrior ran after Artie to a motorboat they'd tied to the 'No Trespassing' sign.

When the phone rang that evening, Hannah answered it. "I'd like to talk to your mother or father," the voice said. Hannah knew it was Artie Spearrin.

"I think you can talk to me," Hannah insisted hotly.

"All right," Artie mumbled. "Listen, I didn't mean to mess up those Indian graves. I mean, like, I was dancing and yelling, but Dave, he's the only one who touched anything. I'm sorry."

"Go on, Artie." It was Mama on the extension phone in the kitchen. Her voice was soft and understanding.

Hannah waited, praying for the Lord to give Mama wisdom. Mama, like other Christians who had been praying for him, hoped Artie's life would change after Sara's death. The Parmenter family had heard that Artie had asked Jesus into his life and was going to church in Foxcroft.

"Mrs. Parmenter?"

"Yes, Artie?"

"Dave's threatening to sue you folks. Hannah's hound messed his arm up real bad. He thinks I'm going to testify for him in court. But there's *no way!* I don't lie since I became a Christian. I saw Dave try to grab Hannah's horse. It was self-defense—that's what I'll say."

"Artie," Mama said softly.

Hannah held her breath and listened.

"You need a friend who doesn't get in trouble."

"You're right about that," Artie agreed.

"Why don't you visit us on Beaver Island next week? I'm sure Walt would love to have a guy to go camping with."

"That'd be great." Artie was so full of joy he was almost crying.

Hannah hugged Mama as soon as she hung up. "Oh, Mama, you're a dear!" she cried.

Chapter Eleven

Only Wigwams on the Hills

"Chief Littledeer is back."

"Oh? When I took him to the bus depot the first day you guys were here, he said he might be back." Hannah cocked a curious eyebrow at Lucy. Lucy's tone said there was more to the story.

The girls watched in silence for a few moments late that Tuesday as Professor Frankenmuth and his archaeology students paddled their big canoe away from Papa's pier.

"He brought two friends—Indians from Canada," Lucy said at last.

"Papa says he's surprised that the whole Penobscot tribe from Abnaki Island didn't come over here as soon as that newspaper story got out," Hannah laughed. "Actually, besides Mr. Littledeer, all we've seen is two local guys pretending to be Indians."

Out of the corner of her eye, Hannah watched Walt and Artie load camping gear onto Walt's pickup. She decided not to tell Lucy that one of the 'local guys' was Artie.

"These fellows are Micmac Indians from New Brunswick. They showed up a few hours before we packed our tools to leave for good. Chief Littledeer had arranged earlier with the professor to come back and rededicate the cemetery."

"Does it take more people than just the shaman to rededicate the cemetery after a dig by archaeologists?" Hannah wondered.

Lucy forced a chuckle. "Not really. Mr. Littledeer showed us a copy of an article about you, Mell, and Hunter. It was an Associated Press article that ran in a New Brunswick newspaper."

Hannah understood. The Associated Press had told the story of her discovery of the Pherson china dolls all over North America. "So I guess the others want to see the cemetery, too," Hannah said. *Why is Lucy so uptight?* she worried silently.

"They also came because they can lend support to his ceremony to honor the spirits and the Manitou."

"Oh?" Hannah was surprised at Lucy's familiarity with Native American religion. Lucy had told her weeks earlier that she was a Christian.

Lucy noticed the worry on Hannah's face. "I *am* a Christian," she said softly. "I settled that with the Lord many years ago. Still, I respect my people's heritage."

"Is there something you're not telling me?" Hannah asked.

"The shaman said that they came to return his ancient people to their resting place. He said the spirits are angry."

"Angry? Why would he believe that? He performed a ceremony at the beginning that he said would appease the spirits."

"Ordinarily the shaman would not be concerned,"

Lucy agreed. "He usually just performs a simple ceremony when Doctor Frankenmuth leaves, and he is satisfied. But..."

Lucy paused. She sounded a mite cross.

"But?" Hannah did not like the sound of this.

"As Chief Littledeer and his friends were about to leave, he stumbled over a human skull. It was out by the logging road, many feet from our dig in the old cemetery."

Hannah gasped. "I...I think I know how it got there."

"You know?!"

"Well, I only *think* so. Go on—what happened then?"

"The shaman said we had lied to them. He said he would need to rebury his people with a full funeral ceremony after all. He plans a complete funeral ritual. He'll probably finish about sundown."

"I...I'm sorry. I was hoping to see Mr. Littledeer when he came back to Beaver Island again," Hannah stammered.

She then told Lucy about how Artie Spearrin's former pal, Dave, ran at her with the skull, and how he tried to grab Ebony's bridle, and how Hunter bit him in defense. But Hannah was careful not to mention Artie's name.

"Well, that does put things in a different light," Lucy said. She had worried that Hannah or Walt had something to do with the misplaced skull.

Hannah sighed. "It's too late now to catch Mr. Littledeer before he leaves, probably. What should we do? I wish I would have driven over and told you guys about the boys right away this morning."

Lucy tried to smile. "There's nothing we can do but call the professor in the morning and ask him to explain what happened. He'll know how to contact the chief."

"You guys want a whole pound of bacon?" Mama asked. She frowned at Walt.

"But, Mama," Walt protested, "the blueberries aren't ripe yet."

"So you and Artie are having biscuits and bacon in the woods instead of blueberry pancakes." Mama smiled, and she seemed amused.

"We'll be hungry," Walt complained.

"You ate like wolves at supper," chuckled Mama.

"We worked like *dogs* to build that wigwam on the back of Bald Hill—didn't we, Artie?"

"Sure did," Artie agreed, but he clearly didn't want to get into the argument between Walt and his mother.

"Tell you what," Mama said quietly. "Hannah, Lucy, and Mell are tenting on the back of the island. They'll be using the old platform where the loggers had their tent. So why don't I give each of you half a pound of bacon, a tube of biscuit dough, and a small jar of honey? Fair enough?"

"Very fair," agreed Hannah, pleased with this turn of events.

"Guys eat more..." Walt stopped, seeing that Lucy was listening. "Fair enough," he agreed with a sigh. Walt didn't want to point out that two guys might eat as much as three girls.

"I like your buggy, Hannah!" The sun was setting far down Moosehead Lake when Lucy climbed onto the seat of the open, four-wheeled carriage next to Hannah. Mell and Hunter hopped into the back.

"Thanks," Hannah said, giving her horse the signal to go. "Papa found it stored in a barn outside Laketon. It hadn't been used for seventy-five years. Ebony learned to pull it right away."

"That's a long time," Lucy agreed. "Y'know, on my island, Prince Edward Island, it hasn't been that long since folks traveled by horse and buggy. My folks can remember when a lot of older people still used them. Life moves slower there, even today."

"Really?" Hannah let Ebony walk across the pasture, picking his way amongst the stones. In her mind, she could see Anne Shirley and Gilbert Blythe as they rode in a buggy behind a trotting horse along the beautiful P.E.I. seaside. *Anne of Green Gables* and *Anne of the Island*—these tales had seemed so long ago and far away. Yet here she was riding in a buggy with Lucy—Lucy of the *real* island, P.E.I.

"You said you'd tell me about your name someday," Hannah said at last. She and Lucy had just moved the cedar bars in the old stone wall so Ebony could pull the buggy through into the forest.

"The French part, the Indian part, or the English part?" Lucy laughed.

"The Indian part!" Mell cried from the back, where she was sitting on a cushion.

"All three," said Hannah. "LaVerdiere is such a pretty family name."

"Well," Lucy sighed, "my name in full, is Lucille Maude LaVerdiere."

Hannah caught her breath. "You were named after Lucy Maud Montgomery, who wrote the *Anne* stories!" she squealed.

"I've seen the movie!" Mell shouted.

"'Anne with an *e*,'" Lucy quoted, her eyes sparkling. "So I got Lucille—Lucy with an *e*. And my middle name is spelled with an *e*, M-a-u-d-e. My mother, who was born on the very day L. M. Montgomery died, decided to give me all *e's*."

"That's only the English part," Mell said. "What about the Indian part?"

"Well," Lucy remarked slowly, "the Indian part of me and the French part go together, I guess. Hundreds of years ago, a trader named Guillaume de la Verdiere came to Canada from France. The French called the land New France in those days. LaVerdiere, like many French settlers, married an Indian wife. Nearly every LaVerdiere in Eastern Canada has married an Indian bride for ten generations. So I guess I'm Abnaki Micmac Indian, with a French name and a French ancestor.

"What's this?" Lucy cried suddenly. "It wasn't here when I rode across the island earlier this afternoon."

In the bushes on the side of Bald Hill, just above the logging road, was a crude hut of poles and fir boughs. Walt's truck was parked next to it.

"Walt's wigwam, I'd say," said Hannah.

The boys appeared just then, pushing aside a tarp which made their door.

Lucy waved cheerfully. "Hi, guys!"

"Arf!" cried Hunter.

"Have fun!" the guys called back. Ebony trotted on, and Walt and Artie were soon out of sight.

Dusk had begun to settle across the woodland when Hannah, Mell, and Lucy finally found the old wooden platform where a cabin once stood. She lit

Papa's gas lantern, and the three girls found themselves inside a cozy glow of light. The loggers had driven steel spikes along the wood floor's rough edges, so the girls put their tent up easily without needing stakes.

"What're those big mounds?" Mell asked.

Lucy had gone inside with the lantern to roll out their sleeping bags. Mell and Hannah found that their eyes were adjusting to the darkness as they fed and tethered Ebony for the night.

"Brush piles," Hannah said. She peered at several large mounds in the distance, just beyond the old burial ground.

"Bushes?" Mell asked.

"No. *Brush*—tree limbs, branches and stuff, left when the loggers cut pine and fir trees. Walt piled up even more when he cut firewood."

"Oh. Looks like wigwams t' me," Mell said. "Kinda like the one Walt and Artie built beside Bald Hill."

"Well, they do look a little like wigwams," Hannah admitted nervously. To tell the truth, she was not happy with the idea that they might have unknown neighbors out here in the dark woods. But Hannah was determined not to let their imaginations fool them. She had seen shapes in the dark before that proved to be quite ordinary objects in the daylight.

Chapter Twelve

Almost Persuaded

Lucy heard it first, while Hannah and Mell still snored in their sleeping bags. She recognized the chant, for she had heard it at her Indian grandmother's funeral:

"Ahh na na mei, kei loosi too gra na. Ahh na na mei, kei loosi too gra na. Ahh na na mei, kei loosi too gra na..." This chant had begun at dawn. It went on and on and on.

"Hannah?"

Hannah stirred.

"Listen! Let's crawl outside," Lucy whispered.

"What? What's that?" Mell was frightened.

"The Micmac Indian chant of the dead. The shaman didn't leave yesterday, after all, I guess."

The girls wriggled outside, then squirmed past the tent platform on their hands and knees.

"Ruff!" rumbled Hunter, who had followed them outside.

"Shush!" Hannah clamped her hound's snout shut. She hugged Mell as the child trembled silently.

The old Indian cemetery was only about two hundred yards away. Someone had built a small hut on the gravel ridge above the cemetery—right where Hannah and Mell had seen a brush pile in the dark.

"A wigwam?" Hannah asked.

"A *real* wigwam, and it wasn't there yesterday afternoon," whispered Lucy. "It was nearly dark when we got here last night, so we didn't notice it. Since it's built of brush, it blends right in with the forest."

"Last night in the dark it looked just like another pile of brush," Hannah added.

Chief Littledeer wore a feather headdress, held in place by a band of colored glass beads. His robe, which fell to his knees, was fine buckskin, bleached to a beautiful off-white. Long fringes decorated every seam. Below each knee was wrapped another beaded band, like the one across his forehead. Moosehide moccasins and deerskin leggings trimmed with thongs completed his outfit.

As the shaman danced and chanted, he waved a tasseled gourd rattle in one hand. In his other hand, he held a long-stemmed peace pipe, called a calumet. Feathers hung from its bowl and stem. From time to time, he would blow smoke across the graves to make peace with what he believed to be angry spirits of the dead. Then he danced some more.

"He believes his own spirit is in the smoke from the calumet," Lucy said. "He wants to satisfy the spirits he thinks are angry because that skull was tossed carelessly on the ground."

"Will...will he hurt us?" Mell whimpered.

"Of course not," Hannah said. "Chief Littledeer is only conducting his religious ceremony." Deep

inside, though, Hannah was a little afraid, for Lucy
had said just yesterday that the chief was angry.

Two other Native Americans were with Chief
Littledeer. They sat on logs. One thumped on a
drum as the chief sang and danced. The other, with
a modern camera, snapped pictures.

"I...I'm going to talk with Chief Littledeer,"
Hannah suddenly declared. He had been so nice
when she took him to the bus in Laketon. She didn't
want him to leave the island angry.

"D...don't leave me, Han," worried Mell.

"You just hang onto Hunter," Hannah said
firmly.

"Hannah, what?" Lucy raised a worried eyebrow.

"Trust me. I'm not going to...to desecrate the
cemetery," Hannah said. *Desecrate.* She was not
sure she'd used the right word, but Lucy seemed to
understand.

The dancing and chanting had now stopped,
and the shaman, with his two friends, sat on a log
by his hut. The three were chatting quietly, nodding
toward the girls' tent.

Hannah circled wide around the Indian cemetery, to be sure she wouldn't offend the shaman by
disturbing the bones of his ancestors. "Sir—Chief
Littledeer?" she said at last, when she stood in front
of him.

"Yes. Speak, child—Hannah." He remembered
her and answered in the quiet, kind voice she
remembered from before.

"I wish to apologize...some of our neighbors...local boys...messed with...with the graves of
your people."

The chief looked confused. "No! The professor
and his students did!" He frowned and nodded
toward where Lucy stood with Mell and Hunter,

next to the tent. It clearly troubled him that his friend the professor would be so careless in his work.

Dear Lord, help me answer wisely, Hannah prayed silently.

"I found a *human* skull. It was way over there!" The shaman emphasized 'human,' and he did not say 'Indian.'

Hannah decided that he was trying to say that desecrating an Indian cemetery is an offense to all humanity, not just Indians. He seemed to expect her to realize that if it is wrong to desecrate the graves of Christians, it is also wrong to desecrate the graves of these Native Americans who worshiped nature.

Hannah took a deep breath. "That skull was dropped by a trespasser from the mainland. When I tried to protect the cemetery, he attacked me and tried to hurt me. So my dog bit him."

"Oh?" The chief seemed surprised. "In that case, I owe Miss LaVerdiere an apology. I was so upset...I should have listened when the students said they didn't know what happened." He rose and walked toward Lucy.

Hannah noticed that Hunter wagged his tail in welcome as the chief approached. Mell noticed it, too, and she let go of Lucy's hand.

After apologizing again to Lucy for saying that she and her classmates had lied, Chief Littledeer smiled at Hannah. "Does Beaver Lodge serve meals to transients?"

"Transients? Oh, you mean people just passing through?" asked Hannah. "Yes, once in a while— Mama charges five dollars," she quickly added.

"Well, my friends and I have been fasting, and we haven't eaten since dawn yesterday. We're so hungry we'd fight a bear for a hive of wild bees. We have a six-hour drive back to our home on the Miramichi River in New Brunswick."

"You're not taking the bus?" Hannah was surprised.

"No. Gil LeViolette brought his new pickup." The chief nodded toward his friends, who already were walking toward the girls' tent to join them.

✳ ✳ ✳ ✳ ✳ ✳ ✳

"Maybe I'd better trot Ebony over to the lodge and tell Mama to expect three extra guests for breakfast." The chief and his two friends had gone back to their temporary wigwam and were busy packing their things.

"Don't bother." Lucy smiled and jerked her thumb toward an aluminum boat tied to a tree by the lake. "A motorboat will outrun a horse any day. Let's have *our* breakfast."

✳ ✳ ✳ ✳ ✳ ✳ ✳

Hannah was surprised to find Chief Littledeer and his friends still at Beaver Lodge when she, Mell, and Lucy trotted up in Ebony's buggy some time later. The men sat in the living room, and they were having a serious, yet friendly, chat with Papa.

"Hello, Hannah—hi, Lucy and Mell," Chief Littledeer greeted the girls as they stepped into the living room.

The chief sat in a wide-armed maple rocker by the new stone fireplace. Hannah thought the chief looked like he belonged at Beaver Lodge in a special way as he sat there in his Indian clothes, with Hunter's basset mama, Missy, draped across his feet.

"A handsome hound, but an old, old one," Mr. Littledeer murmured.

"Yes," Hannah agreed. "She's a beautiful dog." To tell the truth, Hannah hadn't paid much attention to Missy since Hunter had grown big enough to follow her around the island.

"She'll be off to the happy hunting ground before the north winds blow, I'm afraid."

"Yes." Hannah agreed with the chief, but she was unsure. A dog going to the happy hunting ground was a new idea, and she was quite sure it did not come from the Bible. Hannah smiled and said no more, since Mr. Littledeer seemed to wish to talk more with Papa.

But then she got an idea. "Excuse me, please," she said politely. Then she hurried toward the stairs to her room.

Hannah quickly found the nice camera Mama and Papa had bought for her twelfth birthday. It was loaded with high-speed black-and-white film, just right for preserving the memory of a really perfect summer. And since it was high-speed film, Hannah knew she could snap pictures of the folks downstairs in the living room without disturbing their chat with flashes.

"So you had to stay overnight?" Hannah heard Papa ask the shaman, as she returned to the living room with her camera.

"The spirits were very angry. A skull was thrown about like a toy."

"I understand," said Papa. "If someone were treating my family cemetery like that, I'd be pretty upset, too."

Hannah slipped quietly around the room. Without using her flash, she focused on Chief Littledeer, framing him and Missy as he smiled for her.

"Miss LaVerdiere, you are of our people." The chief smiled again, nodding at Lucy.

"I am, sir," she said. "I, too, was shocked when you found that skull."

"But you...you saw no need for us to appease the spirits?" Chief Littledeer searched Lucy's eyes.

"I no longer believe as you believe," Lucy said.

"And?" The chief still looked at Lucy. He seemed to expect her to say more.

"Now that I am a Christian..." Lucy began.

"Now that you are a Christian," the shaman said, finishing what Lucy began, "you believe that the spirits or souls are already gone from the bones anyway."

"Yes, Chief. The Bible teaches that, and I believe it with all my heart," Lucy agreed.

"A Roman chief once told Paul the apostle, 'You almost persuade me to become a Christian,'" Chief Littledeer said. "Professor Frankenmuth showed me that from his Bible one time. Like that Roman, I still choose to doubt." The chief rose. "We have many miles to go before we sleep. Mrs. Parmenter?" he spoke toward the kitchen.

"Yes?" Mama stepped in from the kitchen, smiling.

"That was the best breakfast I've ever eaten in this land between Maine's two great rivers," Chief Littledeer chuckled. "If your skill as a cook had been known in the old days, our people would have become friends many years ago!"

The chief's friends also thanked Mama for their breakfast. Then they strode out, hurrying for their boat, which they'd tied up at Beaver Lodge's dock.

"Mr. Littledeer is a well-learned man," Papa remarked moments later, watching the boat pull away from the dock.

"Why do you say that, Papa?" Hannah asked.

"Religion, philosophy, history—he's studied it all."

"Do you think he'll ever become a Christian, Papa?"

"We can only pray. I believe the Lord is dealing with his heart." Papa was thoughtful for a moment. "Professor Frankenmuth has been talking with the chief about the Gospel."

Lucy beamed. "I was so glad to find that out. I want so much for my Micmac people—all people— to know how much God loves them. In recent weeks, I've really felt like the Lord is wanting me to share Jesus with those who don't know Him. He seems to be telling me to look around and start with those I know best, like my own people."

Hannah was excited. "God must have used meeting Chief Littledeer to help you see this."

Lucy nodded. "More than you can know."

"I think we should stop to pray for the chief right now," said Papa.

Chapter Thirteen

Good-bye
to Missy

"Good things often come in small packages," Hannah was fond of hearing Mama say. So when Walt brought her a package no larger than a ring box from the Laketon Post Office, Hannah expected something very good, indeed. The package had a Charlottetown, P.E.I., postmark. Lucy LaVerdiere lived in Charlottetown, on Hannah's second-favorite island (though she'd never been there). So Hannah easily guessed who sent her the tiny box.

Ever since she received the beautiful green jade Vietnamese potbellied pig from her friend, Marie Janeki, in New York, Hannah had learned to savor unwrapping packages from friends. She did not tear into this one all at once, like a little kid. Instead, she unwrapped each part by itself as she relaxed, enjoying the lake breezes as she sat on the porch glider. Hannah carefully read the note she found in the outer wrapping:

Thank you so much for the lovely photos of you and Hunter, and for the beautiful shot of Chief

*Littledeer with Hunter's mama, Missy. The fireplace
makes such a perfect background for them.*

Hannah examined the paper and found it bor-
dered with a pretty oceanside scene of gulls perched
on a post by a pier.

P.S.,

said a note at the bottom,

the chief's address is:

> *Mr. LeRoi Littledeer*
> *37 River Road*
> *Miramichi, New Brunswick, CANADA E2 B2*

Hunter's basset mother, old and feeble, her pup-
bearing days long gone, now spent most days sleeping in a basket behind the kitchen's wood-burning
range. On hot days, Mama would help Missy outside to pant herself to sleep in the porch shade.
Though Hannah loved Missy, she had had little
time for her. Since the day Hannah rescued Hunter
from drowning when he was a pup, *he* had been her
companion. No doubt the chief had been right,
Hannah considered. Missy would not live long. As
Hannah thought about these things, she felt a pang
of shame in her heart.

Next, Hannah slit the tape on the inner wrapping with her fingernails. *What is this?* Hannah slid
an exquisite carving of a hound from the box. It was
crafted from beautiful pink conch shell. "GENUINE
MICMAC INDIAN CRAFT," read a slip of paper
beneath the carved dog. She turned it over:

*M. Gilbert LeCroix is P.E.I.'s foremost Native North
American artist. He works mostly in North Atlantic
clam, oyster, and scallop shells. Occasionally M.
LeCroix's travels take him to the tropics. Here he
finds conch and other exotic shells for his handicraft.*

Hannah put the note down and went to find
Missy in her basket behind the kitchen stove. She

lay silent, and Hannah easily imagined that if Missy were human she'd be white as death. Occasionally Missy would take a breath, long, deep, and labored. Then she would cease breathing for what seemed forever.

❀ ❀ ❀ ❀ ❀ ❀ ❀

"Why don't you and Walt mourn Missy by digging her grave?" Mama asked the next morning. She tousled Hannah's strawberry blonde snarls.

Hannah knew better than to suggest a funeral. Dogs don't die in hope of a resurrection. Still, Mama could show just a bit more sympathy, Hannah thought.

The west side of Bald Hill was where the setting sun warmed Beaver Island last each day. Hannah and Walt decided to bring Missy there, even though they were not sure just where the property line was between Papa's land and the old Sampson place.

"Let's dig her grave over there," Hannah cried. She pointed to a spot on the far side of the blueberry barrens, where the wild strawberries grew thickest.

"Whatcha diggin'?" Sam Sampson had walked up to investigate the dirt he'd seen flying from Hannah's shovel. It was her turn to dig, and Walt was stretched out in the grass beside Missy's basket. Sam did not snarl at Hannah as he had when he discovered that Hunter had killed several of his fancy potbellied pigs.

"A grave." Hannah leaned on her shovel, wiping her sweating cheek with her sleeve. "Are we on your property?"

"Yes, but that's okay." Then oddly Sam added, "I don't want no trouble with the cops."

"Why would there be trouble?" Walt sat up now, puzzled at their neighbor's strange remark.

"You've already had trouble enough, diggin' up that cemetery. Are y' buryin' enny Indian bones?"

Hannah smiled in spite of Sam's serious manner. No doubt Mell and little Paul's reports to their parents about the goings-on at the Indian cemetery had made things seem worse than they really were. "No sir," she chuckled. "It was the summer archaeology class from the University of Maine that dug up the bones. Then a couple of boys from Laketon caused trouble for themselves by messing with a skull."

"Hannah, get to the point, please!" Walt was peeved that his sister seemed to be dragging her story out.

"Oh—we're burying a dead dog," Hannah finished.

"Not Hunter, I hope. I've come to love that ol' houn'!"

"Not Hunter. His mama, Missy." Hannah went from laughter to tears in one breath.

"Girls!" Walt muttered, disgusted at his sister's sniffles.

"Half the world is girls and women," said Sam, wisely defending Hannah.

"Yeah, I know. Sorry, sis."

"By the way, your Hunter's gonna be a pop right soon," Sam added, sort of as an afterthought.

"How soon?" Hannah forgot about Missy for the moment, where she lay cold and still in an old wicker clothes basket, wrapped in the ratty quilt which had been her bed.

"Soon enough so's we could use a basket." Sam was never bashful about borrowing. He nodded toward Missy's basket. "My beagle, Helen, is due enny day now."

Walt shrugged. "Bury Missy in just her blanket? What do y' say, Han?"

"Fine with me."

Though she never would have admitted it, the thought of not having to dig such a large hole in the hot sun seemed good to Hannah. She mopped her tears on her sleeve and went back to digging Missy's grave. Hannah knew she would miss Missy terribly. The faithful basset was her Hunter's mama. But she also knew that, as a dog, Missy was not to be mourned over the same way one would mourn the death of a human.

"My turn," Walt said after a while. He took the long-handled spade as Hannah, panting, dropped onto an old log nearby. Walt took just a couple shovelfuls of dirt, then rested on the handle. "That's a switch," he remarked, nodding to where the old Sampson place rose over the top of Bald Hill.

"What do y' mean?" Hannah was puzzled.

"Here we are digging a dog grave on Sam Sampson's property. Only a few months ago he'd have been over here cussing, and threatening to sue or have us arrested."

"Yeah, I know." Hannah was thoughtful, awe-struck, almost, at the change in Sam and Judy Sampson and their children. "The Lord changes people, you know," she said finally.

"That's for sure," Walt said, taking another shovelful of dirt.

Hannah smiled through her tears. "Y'know what else?"

"What?" Walt wondered.

"Chief Littledeer loved Missy. I think it was love at first sight."

"We got puppies, seven of 'em!" Paul Sampson had never before been to Beaver Lodge before mid-morning. So the entire Parmenter family knew what was up when Paul sprang onto the porch at 6:30, just as they were finishing breakfast. "Born some-time las' night!" he squealed.

"I'll bet they're sweet," Hannah said. "Do they all look like beagles?"

"Better'n beagles. An' they got longer legs than beagles, like Hunter. My mom says you can have free!" Paul held up three fingers.

"Three?" Mama asked. "I guess we'll pass—tell your mom 'no thanks.'"

"This island is not big enough for seven puppies, plus two adult dogs," Papa said firmly, as soon as Paul raced off for home. He carried his dishes to the sink, then strode across the dining room to his office to work on his business accounts.

It was nearly ten o'clock when Hannah finally found a break from helping Mama feed breakfast to their hungry hotel guests. Paul had been to the lodge three times that morning to give up-to-the-minute reports on the progress of the newborns. Mell came twice. On her second appearance, during Beaver Lodge's busiest time of the day, Hannah sat Mell on a kitchen stool. Hannah put Mell to work paring potatoes to earn the pancakes, sausage, and orange juice she and Paul had wolfed down between excited shouts about the puppies. The puppies' mama, Helen, couldn't have been happier herself, Hannah decided. She smiled to herself as she hurried upstairs to get her camera.

"C'mon, Mell," Hannah cried, moments later, bounding down the steps.

"Coming, Miz Parmenter?" Mell asked Mama.

"I'd love to!" Mama said, and she truly meant it.

"But my hotel guests need me here. Tell your mother I'll be over to see the puppies another time."

"The puppies are so darling!" Judith Sampson knelt by the box where seven calico-patched pups squirmed and squealed. They crawled over one another as they struggled to get their first breakfast on earth.

"They are beautiful little beagles, aren't they?" Hannah said.

Quick mental math told her that the pups were ¼ Labrador, ¼ basset, and ½ beagle. But they were all purebred Beaver Island hound dogs, Hannah thought, as she took pictures, using the camera's flash to light the shadows in the deep box where Helen nursed her babies.

Hannah remembered Papa's opinion of this remarkable birth of beagle babies. She wondered if Mr. Sampson would agree with Papa, or decide to keep all seven. Hannah was glad, though, that she'd given Sam the basket for Helen. In her heart, she knew that Missy would have wanted it saved for her new grandchildren.

Dear Chief Littledeer,

Hannah wrote, two weeks later. The photos of the puppies had come back from the developer, along with extra prints of Missy and LeRoi Littledeer in front of Beaver Lodge's fireplace. She had the pictures spread on a table in her room as she wrote.

Missy—that's the dog in the picture with you—is dead. I thought you'd want to know. The pups in the color photos are Missy's grandchildren and also Hunter's kids. Since I know you like hounds, I'm sending you some pictures. Mell and Paul want to give several puppies away. Too bad you live too far away to take one.

Your friend,
Hannah

Chapter Fourteen

Walt's Confession

"Hey! That's a neat medallion!" Walt admired Hannah's handcrafted conch-shell hound, which she'd strung on a stout nylon cord and hung around her neck. "Goes nice with your shirt."

"Thanks!" Hannah smoothed down her new cream-colored T-shirt. "And I like your beads." Actually, Hannah *did* like Walt's beads. But she was not sure if she liked this kind of jewelry on a guy. Sure, Hannah had seen plenty of necklaces on guys around Laketon, and on a few guests at their lodge, but somehow necklaces didn't seem to belong on boys. But probably Papa won't say anything unless Walt wears them to church, Hannah decided.

"Where'd you get them?" There was no accusation in Hannah's voice, only friendly curiosity. The beads were beautiful mother-of-pearl, polished to a high luster.

"I polished them on the buffer in the shop and strung them myself. See." Walt slid the necklace around to show the knotted ends of the string. It was new nylon cord, like the cord from Mama's spool in the kitchen drawer, which Hannah had used herself to string her conch-shell hound medallion.

"From Mama's spool?" Again, Hannah was not implying that Walt had done something he shouldn't have. Mama did not mind if Hannah or Walt used her cord, so long as they were not wasteful. They both knew that, of course.

"So??" Walt bristled angrily.

"I'm sorry I asked." Hannah left, truly puzzled by why Walt would get mad over a simple question. *And why had Walt avoided telling where the beads came from?* Hannah worried.

Dear Diary,
Hannah wrote that evening,
Something is dreadfully wrong with Walt, and I'm afraid it has to do with his new beads. Is he afraid I'll make fun of him because he's a boy? Walt knows I love him too much for that!!!! I just hope he doesn't stay mad at me too long.

Hannah prayed that the Lord would help her and Walt love each other as brother and sister. "And if something is bothering Walt," she concluded, "please help him make it right. In Jesus' name, amen."

Hannah had begun her diary months earlier, right after she created her own secret hideout in the barn. It was a cavern deep beneath the hay in the haymow, far back where nobody would disturb it. Hannah had been so busy since she and Mell spotted the Indian vase in the woods that she hadn't come to her secret place very often.

One of her favorite things about her hideout was that it had its own special window, an unused upstairs door which the former owners had put in to unload hay bales with a conveyor. Tonight Hannah pushed this upper door open to view the last rays of the dying sun. Far, far down the lake beyond Mt. Kineo, the sun had sunk from sight. It was not a glorious red sunset this evening, with purple tints streaming along the western horizon. Oh no— tonight the sun sank from sight sadly, quietly as if to say, *Tomorrow the storm.*

> Red skies at night,
> Sailors delight;
> Red skies in the morning,
> Sailors take warning.

Many times Mama had repeated this little rhyme she had learned from Grandma. Usually Hannah heard her mother quote this old saying during a glorious sunset the family was watching across Moosehead Lake from the porch of Beaver Lodge. And always the next day was fair and bright.

Does it follow that tomorrow will be foul when there is no red sunset? Hannah asked herself half aloud. *And did Walt steal those beads?* Even some folks you believe would do no wrong may let you down.

That night Hannah lay awake long past midnight. She knew Walt earned money by doing jobs for Papa around the island. Papa had paid him ten dollars a truckload for cutting treetops into firewood and hauling them home.

But most of Walt's money went for sports equipment or truck parts. Last winter at Laketon Christian Academy, Hannah had heard of a student caught shoplifting in a drugstore. Walt had come home with some nice stuff lately, too. There had been an expensive watch, which he said he got on sale at half price. Last week he displayed a nice pocketknife, an Uncle Henry model with a genuine staghorn handle.

But Walt said he polished the mother-of-pearl beads himself. Would he make up such a story? It frightened Hannah to think he would.

Still, there were antique shops around Laketon that carried old stuff in rough shape to sell to tourists. They paid fancy prices for what Aunt Theresa called "junk." Then people spent even more money fixing it up.

Did Walt just fill his pockets with old, valuable handmade beads he'd seen in an antique shop?

"Is that *all* you took?"

Walt would never lie to Mama, Hannah knew.

"No, Mama. I took the beads, too."

Hannah held her breath. Walt had left the barn that morning several minutes ahead of her. She was outside the kitchen's screen door now, lugging a pail of Molly's fresh milk.

"You'll have to give them back."

"But, Ma, I don't know how to find the man. He's gone back to Canada!"

So that was it! Walt had stolen from some guy who'd brought in a truckload of stuff from Canada to sell to tourists and take advantage of higher American money values. Most of the local merchants resented these traveling peddlers, who sold right out of the backs of their pickups and paid no local taxes. Kids caught stealing from them were usually not even arrested, because the peddlers would seldom stay in Maine long enough to testify in the Foxcroft Circuit Court. Walt knew this, of course. Hannah knew this, too. Even some of the kids in the Christian school found it funny. *But stealing is stealing,* Hannah thought, filled with sadness that her brother would do such a thing.

"Well," sighed Papa just then, "he couldn't possibly have known you took them."

Hannah could see Papa at the kitchen counter pouring himself a cup of coffee. *Is Papa saying it's all right to steal if the owner doesn't know you stole?* Hannah could not believe her ears. *God knows,* she thought, hot tears coming to her eyes.

"Come in, Hannah," Papa said pleasantly, spying her waiting outside. "There's a lesson here for you, too."

"But, Mama, I didn't really *steal* anything," Walt protested as Hannah walked in.

"He's right, you know," Papa agreed. "It's like Mell Sampson's vase."

On the table on a paper towel were several very old human bones. Next to the bones lay Walt's new necklace of antique beads.

"I got these one day when I was hauling wood from over there, before the university students came," Walt confessed. "I picked them out of the dirt the woodchuck threw out. At the time, I had no reason to believe the beads belonged in somebody's grave." Walt looked searchingly at Papa. "I could just bury them where I found them in that Indian graveyard, but the bones were not in the grave when the shaman did his sacred dance. They were still in my room."

"LeRoi Littledeer's dance did nothing good nor bad for the bones of people who died hundreds of years ago," Papa said thoughtfully. "When folks die, their soul goes either to heaven or hell, where they wait the resurrection. The shaman's dance to appease the spirits he believes guard those graves appeased only himself and those who believe in the power of his dance. You said one of Mr. Littledeer's friends was taking pictures of the ceremony," Papa said to Hannah.

"Oh!" exclaimed Hannah. "He's going to show his tribe the pictures so they will see how he rededicated the graves."

"Exactly," Papa agreed. "By seeing the pictures, his friends in Canada will feel they had a share in the rededication. But the Bible teaches that the shaman's dance means nothing to the souls of the people buried there, though Chief Littledeer and his people believe it does."

"The bones and the beads *do* belong back in the graves," Walt said, relieved. "I sure wouldn't think it's right for someone to just help themselves to stuff buried in a grave in my family cemetery, even a hundred years from now." Walt turned to Hannah. "Han," he said, "don't you have the chief's address? I think I should write him and explain what happened."

"You do that!" Hannah exclaimed, giving her big brother a bear hug. "But what about Mell's vase?" It was Hannah's turn to worry.

"Last time I talked with Professor Frankenmuth he had his doubts if that vase even belonged to the Indian cemetery," Papa said mysteriously.

Chapter Fifteen

Anne of the Island

"Mama," teased Hannah one day, "why can't we paint the gables of Beaver Lodge green?" Ever since Lucy from Prince Edward Island had become Hannah's special big sister, Hannah's head had simply swirled with her imaginations of Lucy Maud Montgomery's famous *Anne of Green Gables*. Hannah had also read *Anne of Avonlea*. In *Avonlea*, Hannah found herself quite in love with the more mature girl of Green Gables, who at last had returned home to P.E.I. after several years away at college on the mainland.

"'Why can't we?' You mean, 'Why don't we?'" Mama warned gently. "*Can't* sounds a little pushy."

"Oh, I really didn't mean to be pushy." With just a wistful bit of sadness Hannah added, "I've been reading about..."

"...Anne Shirley. 'Anne with an *e*,'" Mama guessed, finishing Hannah's sentence.

"But it's more than just reading," Hannah insisted. "In *Anne of the Island*, Anne comes back to the dearest place on earth to her."

"I understand, darling." Mama tousled Hannah's strawberry hair. "I read all of the *Anne* books when I was about your age." She whistled a line from an old song about a girl with strawberry blonde hair.

"It's wild carrot hair, like Anne Shirley's, from now on," Hannah corrected. "And my personal blossom is Queen Anne's lace."

"Well, we've certainly got enough of it on *this* island, that's for sure," Mama agreed. She peered out the window to where the white, lacy blossoms of the wild carrot plant marched up the stony hillside pasture toward the pine forest. Molly, the family cow, and Hannah's horse, Ebony, ate their grass in this pasture, ignoring the wild carrots with their white Queen Anne's lace flowers as unfit even for their beastly appetites.

"Your hair may be pink, like the carrot root," Mama said, exasperated. "But if you don't stop talking in riddles, mine will soon be white, like the blossom."

"Oh, Mama!" Hannah hugged her mother. "It's not as bad as that. I just get in these dreamy moods once in a while."

"I guess you're lonely, now that Lucy's gone back to Prince Edward Island," Mama sympathized. "I remember how lonely our house seemed after *my* big sis—your Aunt Theresa—left to marry Joe."

"And do you know who Lucy is named for?"

"Let me guess," Mama chuckled. "Lucy Maud Montgomery, who wrote *Anne of Green Gables* and *Anne of the Island.*"

Hannah brightened. "I am Anne of Beaver Island."

"But Papa and I named you Hannah, after the mother of the great prophet Samuel, in the Bible." Mama pretended to sound worried.

"Hannah and Anne are just different spellings of

the same Bible name, like Mary and Marie," said Hannah. "The dictionary says so. They both mean *grace.*"

"I guess you're right," Mama agreed. "Grace—I like that. Jesus was 'full of grace and truth,' the Bible says, and He was gracious too."

Hannah was practically aglow now. "Yes, Mama. It's an awesome thing to be named Grace or Anne or Hannah. As for the gables, I'll just have to pretend they're green if we can't paint 'em. I'm turning this island into Anne's island, beginning right now."

᠅ ᠅ ᠅ ᠅ ᠅ ᠅ ᠅

"Aunt Theresa," Hannah cried, "may I take the cushions from your old porch glider down to the public wharf?" Hannah glanced at a seldom-used glider rusting beneath the branches of Aunt Theresa's apple tree.

"Of course. Just bring 'em back."

"Thanks, Auntie!" Hannah hurried off, her copy of *Anne of the Island* tucked under one arm.

Hannah's entire family had taken Papa's big motorboat to Laketon for Sunday school and church that morning. It was one of those rare summer weekends when all of Beaver Lodge's tourist guests left on Saturday. No more guests were expected until late Sunday evening, so Mama, Papa, Walt, and Hannah were spending the afternoon with Aunt Theresa and Uncle Joe. Aunt Theresa had done herself proud for Sunday dinner, baking Hannah's very favorite dessert, fresh raspberry pie, from the patch of plump berries in the Boudreaus' backyard.

Hannah was in a far-off world as she lay on the dock. She spied the afternoon sun's reflection off the copper roof of Beaver Lodge three miles across the water, and it seemed to Hannah that she was seeing Anne's Green Gables through the mists of Northumberland Strait.

The clack of a wooden croquet ball against another ball broke Hannah's reverie about Beaver Island and Prince Edward Island for just a minute. "I'm gonna *send* your ball clear under the backyard fence for a ho-o-o-o-ome run!" came Caylin Coulson's gleeful squeal. Caylin's family lived next door to Aunt Theresa. When she learned at Sunday school that Walt and Hannah would spend the afternoon there, she made plans to join them for a game of lawn croquet. Walt and Hannah liked to have her play, even if her sparkling personality added more to the game than her athletic skill did.

Usually a yard game on a summer Sunday afternoon would have been just what Hannah liked. But with only three chapters left to read, Hannah decided to finish her book first.

Now, down on the dock with her very favorite lake stretching out before her, Hannah found herself doing more thinking than reading. Anne Shirley had seen Prince Edward Island's red clay shores from the deck of a ferry boat after years away earning a degree at Redmond College in Nova Scotia. Hannah now watched an excursion boat splash across Moosehead Lake, its paddle wheel sending up a white shower of spray. She pulled her perky straw hat lower across her forehead, squinting into the sun for a better look. Though Hannah guessed most of the women on this boat probably wore jeans—though some did wear straw hats—in her heart's eye she could see them in the ankle-length summer dresses worn in Anne Shirley's day, three-quarters of a century ago.

The water of Moosehead Lake seemed in Hannah's mind to be the Northumberland Strait of the North Atlantic, separating Prince Edward Island from the mainland of Nova Scotia and New Brunswick. The granite rocks that lined the shore of Beaver Island now caught the afternoon sun. With a wee bit of imagination, these rocks became the red shores of P.E.I.

Alone on the dock, Hannah spoke half aloud. "And I shall leave my dear, dear island never again to return. What's to become of me?" That she was growing up sometimes made Hannah fearful and excited all at once. She thought of Anne, who nearly gave her heart to a man she did not really, truly love; who almost lost her dear Gilbert Blythe to typhoid fever. But she also thought of the neat people Anne had met when she left Green Gables, all the new places she visited, the adventures. It would be so exciting to go away from home for a while like Anne and Lucy LaVerdiere, even if it would be a little scary.

"C'mon, Han, we ne-eed another pla-aayer!" Walt's yell from Uncle Joe's backyard interrupted Hannah's contemplations just then. She laid her book down to listen.

"Hannah! Let's go-ooh!"

That Walt! Hannah grumbled. She knew, of course, what the matter was. As enthusiastic and fun as Caylin was, and as good as she was at lots of things, she was no good at sports. Walt had quickly become bored with winning every game of croquet. He needed his sister to liven up the game. But Hannah closed her ears, if ears can close. She went back to her imagining and reading, remembering the events, the people God had brought to her island.

Hannah of Beaver Island, unlike Anne of Prince

Edward Island, hadn't been away from her island for more than a few days at a time. But that didn't mean she hadn't met her share of incredible people, Hannah chuckled to herself. Papa would say that the Lord had sent people to her to help her grow up, right where she lived on Beaver Island. These were people like Professor Frankenmuth, who, with his scientific findings, was busy helping others understand the world. Then came Chief Littledeer, who Hannah discovered she could respect and love even though she did not share his beliefs.

And then there was Lucy. From her, Hannah learned that growing up is a very long process, not even complete when you're nineteen. Of course, Lucy was also Hannah's living link to Green Gables.

Hannah patted her straw hat again. She'd found it in a store in Skowhegan just last week, on a shopping trip with Aunt Theresa. *It suits me well,* Hannah thought. *Anne Shirley wore one like it.*

Anne, Hannah remembered, had come from Nova Scotia as an orphan at age eleven. After seven years at Green Gables, Anne had returned to Nova Scotia to go to college. But, "I'm island to the core," she had told her new friend Philippa.

"Beaver Island is my *home,*" Hannah breathed happily, stretching out on the cushions and trying to nap.

"Queen Anne, herself!" A teasing voice full of mirth and fake dignity woke Hannah from her slumber.

"Hey, Anne of the island," snickered another fake voice.

Hannah opened one eye. In an old peanut butter jar, right beneath her nose, was a big bouquet of Queen Anne's lace, with its homely, cottage-cheese-like blossoms. Hannah had dozed off in solemn bliss. She woke up to this silly banter, and somehow the teasing hurt. Suddenly all the grace that Anne—or Hannah—stood for left her. She seized the Queen Anne's lace, jar and all, and heaved the bouquet into the lake.

Hannah watched Walt and Caylin disappear behind the high board fence separating Uncle Joe's yard from the public wharf. *Am I more mad at them or myself, now?* Hannah groaned. True, they had made fun of her, but they probably didn't *mean* to be mean. The silly bouquet of Queen Anne's lace just made her feel stupid, because she *had* practically been pretending to be Anne on the dock.

Hannah stood up, planning to follow Walt and Caylin and apologize for being so touchy about their joke. Then she saw the sign: Warning—$100 fine for throwing glass bottles into lake. Violators WILL BE prosecuted! Hannah knew that the town of Laketon had passed this stern ordinance just weeks ago, right after a boater was severely injured by broken glass. Spotting the peanut butter jar bobbing out of reach beyond the dock, Hannah knew what she must do.

Soaking wet, she tried to sneak up Aunt Theresa's back stairs to change from her jeans and T-shirt back into the dress she had worn to church that morning.

"Hannah, what...?" Mama spied Hannah, just as she reached the top step.

"Mama, don't say anything to Han. I'll explain." Walt stopped his mother before she could say more about Hannah returning looking like a drowned duck.

When Hannah came back downstairs, Walt and Caylin were waiting for her.

"Sis, I'm sorry. I was mean."

"I'm sorry, too." Caylin kissed Hannah's cheek.

"Apologies accepted," said Hannah. "And I guess I acted like a jerk."

Hannah was Grace once again. While upstairs, she had asked the Lord to take away her hurt feelings, and He had answered her prayer.

Chapter Sixteen

Secret Places of the Heart

A hay bale makes a lovely bookcase, Hannah decided. She settled back luxuriously onto a pile of loose hay, over which she had spread an old quilt too frayed for a guest room.

Hannah surveyed the row of books she felt were so special that only her secret cave was good enough for them: Here were three of L.M. Montgomery's *Anne of Green Gables* books, a three-book set of *Rebecca of Sunnybrook Farm,* five *Little House* tales—she had been reading Laura Ingalls Wilder's stories since first grade and still enjoyed them—and all seven of C.S. Lewis' *Chronicles of Narnia* books. Of course Hannah kept a Bible in her special cavern, a pictorial one Mama and Papa had got her before she even learned to read. Since it was dusty in here, Hannah kept her best leather-bound Bible in the lodge, on the nightstand beside her bed.

"My library." Hannah rolled the words like sacred music over her tongue. When she spoke these words in thankfulness, Hannah knew that God heard her, for from her heart of hearts she was talking to Him.

Using an old broom handle, Hannah pushed open the door above the barnyard. She jammed it in position just wide enough to allow the rosy glow of the setting sun to illuminate her collection of books and photos.

"And my friends." Hannah's eyes fell on an unframed photo of Lucy LaVerdiere, which she had pegged with an old bent nail into a bale of hay. It was a color snapshot of Lucy standing in front of an old, high-gabled house shaded with elms and maples. Penned across the bottom in Lucy's hand was "Green Gables, P.E.I." Next to Lucy's picture was the black-and-white portrait Hannah had taken of Chief Littledeer sitting by the fire with Missy. It looked old-fashioned and romantic, as if the chief had just stepped into Beaver Lodge from another century. His traditional bleached buckskin robe was beautiful, Hannah thought.

Hannah pulled out a handful of letters from where she kept them under the baling twine that tied one of the hay bales. One was from Marie Janeki in New York. Two, both several weeks old, were postmarked "Charlottetown, P.E.I.—Canada Postal." Both of these were from Lucy. Hannah fished out the most recent one and unfolded it into the last rays of the evening sun.

Dear Hannah (or do you prefer Anne?!),

Lucy had written,

The Lord has been dealing with me in some very special ways since returning to P.E.I. I have felt for a long time that God wants me to be a missionary to my own people. But only during my stay on your island (my "other island") have I begun to learn what that means.

What could Lucy mean? Hannah pondered.

We can talk more when I come back to the University of Maine this fall.

Hannah folded Lucy's letter and slipped it back into its place under the twine that tied the hay bale. Lucy was coming back! What times they could have—Hannah, who was just beginning to become a woman, and Lucy.

"Betcha can't lop one through that door!"

Hannah pressed an ear to the outside wall of the barn to hear more. She decided, though, that it might not be smart to stick her head out the upstairs hay door.

"Wanna bet? I got the best arm with a green apple on Moosehead Lake!"

"Don't y' want t' know what you're firing at first?" Hannah heard the voice of the challenger clearly this time. It was Walt. *But who was the other guy?*

"I can bring down a coon at fifty yards, even without a scope." Hannah knew she'd heard *that* male voice before. It was teasing, but with a pleasant mellow ring.

"Just remember," chuckled Hannah's brother, "Pa said we can't touch off our shootin' irons until we get beyond the old stone wall."

Touch off our shooting irons? Oh—Fire our guns. Hannah got that one. It was guy talk, trying to sound tough and rugged and maybe scare her a bit.

"I'm not gonna *shoot* y' chicken out of the hay loft. I'm just gonna peg a couple o' green apples in there and hear her squawk."

"ZING!" A green apple shot through the door into the gathering darkness and plopped into the hay next to Hannah. Two more barely missed the door. A second rocketed inside, bounced off a barn beam, then hit Hannah on the shoulder just hard enough to sting a little.

"Awwk! Puk-puk-puk-puk! Awwk!" Hannah made chicken-in-distress noises.

"You sure that's a chicken roosting up there in the hayloft? Sounds more like a *chick* t' me. I'll bet it's yer sister. You jerk!"

Walt only laughed, and Hannah could hear the crunch of two pairs of boots as the guys strolled off on their coon hunt.

Far, far up in the peak of Papa's barn was a louver vent which could be reached only in summer, when the barn was full of hay nearly to the ceiling. Remembering that the louver had a slat missing, Hannah scrambled out of her cave and scurried up the tiers of baled hay. She reached the louver in time to peek through and see two guys with shotguns climb over the cedar bars of the gate and enter the forest, just as dusk fell.

One guy was Walt. The other one? Hannah got goosebumps when she realized who Walt had tricked into throwing green apples into her private cave. "That Walt!" she said grimly, though not in anger.

In the barn below, Hannah found a large plastic pail used to water the calves. Without turning on the light, she slipped out the side door to a spot just outside the barnyard fence. Here a big, old apple tree leaned over the barnyard. Apples that fell inside the barnyard were quickly eaten by Molly. Mama had assigned Hannah the task of picking up all the green apples that fell outside, out of reach of Molly's long tongue, and tossing them over the fence. "That way," Mama said, "the cow eats the wormy ones, so we have good apples in the fall for applesauce."

But Hannah had neglected her job for some days. Professor Frankenmuth's archaeology class had taken so much of her time lately that the apples were largely forgotten.

It took Hannah only a few minutes to fill her bucket with all the green apples she cared to carry. A few stones, sticks, clumps of grass, and even dried cow pies got mixed in with the apples in Hannah's bucket. When you work in the dark you can never be certain what you're loading up.

※ ※ ※ ※ ※ ※ ※

Hannah was not surprised the next morning to find several green apples in the second floor hall, by the stairs that led to Walt's third-floor bedroom. The boys had returned from their coon hunt near midnight, and she had heard them tramp up the stairs that wound above her bed. She had stifled giggles in her pillow when, moments later, the guys dragged a bed sheet loaded with green apples and who knows what else down two flights of stairs.

"Keep it down, fellers," Hannah heard Papa whisper hoarsely in the night. Papa was mindful of his guests, who were trying to sleep.

Walt did all the barn chores that morning while Hannah helped Mama get breakfast for the guests. Walt's friend, Hannah correctly guessed, had gone with him to the barn to skin the coons. Hannah pretended to be too busy kneading biscuit dough to pay attention when Walt came into the kitchen with a pail of milk—and Mike Wilson!

"Did that air mattress on the floor make your sleeping bag comfortable last night, Michael?" Mama asked cheerfully.

"Ask Walt, Mrs. Parmenter," said Mike. "I slept in his bed."

Uh-oh, thought Hannah.

"Hannah, I...I'm sorry for throwing the green apples. I guess you got me back good, and I had it coming."

"What green apples?" *I'll have my laugh later,* Hannah decided, stifling chuckles that seemed to want to burst inside her.

"Were...weren't you in the barn loft last night around sunset?"

"The loft? Oh, you mean that upper door into the haymow. We've got a chicken that flies up in there when she wants to be off by herself. That's all."

Mike raised an eyebrow. "Well," he said, "somebody must have really had it in for Walt. You ought t' see the mess in his bed!"

Chapter Seventeen

Regions Beyond

"What's *this* about?" Hannah said under her breath. She trudged toward the lodge early one Saturday carrying a pail of Molly's milk. Hannah recognized the big boat pulling up to the dock in the mists of dawn.

It did not surprise her to see Mike Wilson at the wheel of his dad's nearly new boat as it idled up to the dock. Mike had earned money with this boat all summer ferrying tourists, groceries, and baggage to remote cottages along the shore of Moosehead Lake, in places where there were no auto roads.

But Hannah also recognized the cute, petite girl in the boat with Mike. It was Caylin Coulson. *Walt's not going to like this*, Hannah thought. She knew that Walt and Caylin had agreed to just be friends, but still she was afraid it might make Walt feel bad to see Caylin and Mike together.

"Hi, you guys," Hannah called, waving. She hurried inside with the pail of milk. She wanted to finish her chores quickly so she could see what was up.

"Where are you going with Papa's new radio,

Walt?" Hannah spotted Walt hurrying through the living room with the radio's mobile unit as she climbed up on a stool to reach the milk strainer.

She shot a glance at the kitchen shelf where Papa had installed the base unit of the fancy two-way ham radio set. She knew that Papa had bought this radio so he could talk with Mama when he took hunting and fishing parties deep into the Allagash Wilderness. Much more powerful than a CB radio, this ham radio used a tall antenna, which Papa, Walt, and Sam Sampson had set up on Bald Hill just last month. It took Papa more than a year to get a valuable federal ham radio license. Hannah knew that Papa did not take lightly the responsibility of such a radio.

"We're going to Spencer Bay—The City," Walt grinned. "I'm a licensed radio man, too, you know."

"But The City's a long way! Does Papa know?" Hannah said no more to Walt about the radio. She knew that Papa and Walt had studied for the radio test together.

The tiny village of cottages and cabins known jokingly to folks in Laketon as 'The City' was located at the north end of vast Spencer Bay, half the length of Moosehead Lake away. Even with Mr. Wilson's powerful cabin cruiser, it was at least an hour's ride. Hannah, Walt, and their cousins had once taken Papa's big boat clear over to Mt. Kineo, so she was not really surprised that Walt was going with Mike and Caylin to Spencer Bay. In fact, Hannah was relieved that Caylin had come to go along with *both* Walt and Mike.

"It's all right." Mama, who had heard Hannah's worried question about the radio, stepped into the kitchen just then.

"Yes, but I thought..."

Mama held up a hand. "Papa spoke with Mr. Wilson on the phone last night. Mr. Wilson's boat has a safe bracket to hold a radio, so it'll be protected."

"But...but it took Papa so long to get it!" Hannah protested.

"Papa and I talked it over, and we decided that if Walt was going that far down the lake with Mike it would be a good idea for them to have a way to get in touch with home base. You and Walt are worth more to us than any radio." Mama patted Hannah's tousled hair.

"Well, you are certainly becoming careful with us kids," Hannah chuckled. "Walt and I used to make some pretty long trips without a radio."

"That was before..." Mama frowned sadly, not finishing.

"I know." Hannah bent to put the freshly strained milk in the refrigerator. Silently Hannah thought about the three teens who had drowned in Moosehead Lake earlier that summer when a sudden storm swamped their boat. A United States Coast Guard officer on summer patrol had told the TV and newspaper reporters that a radio could have prevented this tragedy.

When Hannah reached the dock after putting away the strainer, Walt and Mike were busy bolting the radio into a bracket in the boat's cabin.

"That Mike!" said Caylin just then. She was busily picking up odds and ends of trash from the boat and stuffing the junk into a garbage bag.

"Be glad you don't have to clean his room," Hannah laughed. She'd seen her brother's room a few times just before his weekly housecleaning for Mama's inspection. It puzzled Hannah that Walt couldn't just keep his room clean all the time, like she did hers. Then he wouldn't have such a mess to pick up every Saturday afternoon. But since it was Walt's mess, Hannah never let it bother her.

"Yeah," sighed Caylin, who had no older brother. "Boys!"

"You get used to 'em," Hannah laughed.

Mike and Walt were still working on the radio. Hannah bent to pick up a shriveled apple core and was about to toss it into Caylin's garbage bag. Then she remembered the green apples Mike had thrown at a certain chicken. Hannah pitched the core through the boat's open cabin door—hard!

"Ouch!" The apple core stung the back of Mike's neck. He jumped, dropping the radio, which Walt had been bolting in place with a screwdriver and pliers.

Walt barely caught the radio. He glared at his sister. "Watch that stuff!"

Dumb, Hannah thought. *That was really dumb.* "I'm going back to the lodge before I do something even stupider," she said aloud, nodding at Caylin to follow her.

"Hey, wait!" Mike hollered after them. He rubbed his neck, grinning. "I guess I deserved that."

"Girls can pitch apples, too," Hannah laughed, relieved that there was no damage and no hard feelings.

"Want t' come along to The City?" Mike asked suddenly. "I've got a customer over there who needs some stuff taken to Laketon. But we've got plenty of room."

"Well, I..." Hannah stammered. "I'll ask Mama."

"Kids who live on the lake!" Mama snapped moments later. Hannah was not surprised to find her mother making sandwiches for the three teens to eat on their boat trip. "Sometimes I think we should have stayed in Skowhegan. At least there, teens don't get to drive off together until they're sixteen."

Mama was like that. She could be especially kind, like now when she made hearty sandwiches without waiting to be asked. But she could tartly express her opinion at the same time she was being nice, if she felt something was not right.

"Here on Moosehead Lake," Mama went on, "any twelve-year-old who can run an outboard motor can tear off into the wild blue yonder without supervision."

"That's right, Mama," Hannah chuckled, remembering that she had been taking a boat to Laketon alone for more than a year. "Papa says..."

"That you're almost a woman," Mama sighed, kissing Hannah's cheek. "And Michael and Walter are both fifteen. So you may go with them, if it's all right with Papa."

※ ※ ※ ※ ※ ※ ※

"Ever been into Spencer Bay before?" Walt asked. Mike held the boat's wheel as the big launch cut through the whitecaps.

"Not as far as The City," Mike admitted. "I've been pretty busy all summer, though. There's a lot o' work on this lake from Memorial Day to Labor Day for a guy with a boat. Tourists rent cabins where there's only jeep trails for miles around. Since most of 'em don't own jeeps, they need someone with a boat to carry their baggage and groceries. Usually I can make a day's pay real easy and never go far from Laketon."

"I bet your parents would rather you stay near home, anyway," Walt chuckled. "I know mine would."

"That's true." Mike shrugged, remembering that

his mom and dad had insisted he prove himself responsible on local runs for a couple months before letting him cross the big lake to Spencer Bay, way north of Beaver Island. "We're really heading for the 'regions beyond' today, man."

"What does he mean by that?" Caylin asked. She and Hannah sat in swivel boat chairs behind the boys, their long hair flying in the breeze as they barreled along. "Isn't that from the Bible?"

Hannah nodded. "We learned about it last Sunday while you visited your grandparents. These missionaries to Ethiopia, John and Mary Stone, told about an African village so remote it was once called 'The Land Beyond the Nile.' They wanted to go where others hadn't been—to the 'regions beyond,' like Apostle Paul did. That way they could tell others about Jesus in places far away from where Christians already lived, just like missionaries in the Bible."

"'The Land Beyond the Nile.' Didn't people used to say that nobody knew how long the Nile River was?" Caylin wondered.

"That was before explorers discovered the source of the Nile, in Ethiopia," Hannah chuckled. "Actually, the Stones say that the village where they work—Sodo, I think it's called—has a good jeep road now, and a church and a hospital."

"I wonder what this place called 'The City' is like." Caylin rolled her eyes in amusement. Before she and her parents moved to Laketon a year ago, they had lived in a big city in Connecticut.

"We'll know soon, at least in an hour or so." Hannah watched Beaver Island for a few moments as it grew smaller behind them. Up ahead, the long line of green forest at the edge of the water didn't seem to be getting any closer. And the shore they were planning to reach was still out of sight beyond a bend in the big bay.

Hannah's mind ran to the events of days just past. The archaeology dig was one of the most exciting things that had ever happened on Beaver Island! She had met Chief LeRoi Littledeer, who needed Jesus just like the people the Stones knew in The Land Beyond the Nile, and just like the Sampsons had when Hannah first met them. "The regions beyond," Hannah murmured aloud, quoting II Corinthians 10:16.

"This really *is* beyond," said Caylin, who had never been past Beaver Island. "What do you suppose we'll see?" Caylin's eyes sparkled with excitement.

"Maybe someone who needs Jesus," Hannah said, her mind still on the Stones.

"Hey, Han, check out that box!" Mike had been listening to the girls talk.

Hannah raised the watertight lid on the storage bin Mike pointed to. "Why, Mike, you did come prepared!" She reached inside and pulled out a handful of paper packets. Each had a Sunday bulletin from Laketon Community Church, a couple of Sunday school papers, and a tract with a gospel message in it. On the packet was stamped, *Mike's Lake Freight. Ph. 865-5555.*

"Do you leave these with everybody?" Hannah asked.

"Yup." Mike grinned. "We even had a family from a summer cottage visit our church because of this. And when I get a chance," he softly added, "I *tell* people about Jesus."

Chapter Eighteen

A Wild Rosie

"Where does Bill O'Brien live?" Mike asked the storekeeper. "He sent me a message to pick up some packages."

Hannah looked around The City Trading Post as she waited for Mike to get directions. The man he was talking to sat behind an old-fashioned mechanical cash register, reading a book and smoking a pipe. The Trading Post was not much more than a cabin itself, with an uneven plank floor and rough, unfinished rafters like the ones in Papa's barn on Beaver Island. A swallow, Hannah noticed, had built her nest on a beam in the far end of the cabin, and she came and went through a hole where the storekeeper hadn't bothered to fix a broken shingle.

The storekeeper stretched and yawned, but he didn't stand to greet his young guests. "He don't live here in The City," he muttered.

The man paused, and Hannah decided just then that they'd probably come clear up Spencer Bay just for a boat ride. *Mike's not going to get a day's pay from this trip,* she told herself.

"I already know that Mr. O'Brien doesn't live here in The City, sir," Mike said pleasantly. "But he said you could tell me where to find his...his farm."

"Farm? He ain't got no farm. What you want with Bill O'Brien anyway? His word to me has always been, 'No visitors.'"

"Sir, Mr. O'Brien has *paid* me already!" Mike was still polite, but now he insisted.

"Paid yuh, huh? Ain't many that deals with him as ever gits paid. But effen he's paid yuh, I guess he wants to see yuh." The storekeeper yawned, and he began to list trails, logging roads, and paths to reach the O'Brien cabin. "'Bout two miles in all, mostly uphill. Good thing yer haulin' stuff out, not in."

"Thanks." Mike strode across the creaky floor toward the door.

"Excuse me, sir," Walt stammered, hanging behind to question the storekeeper. Walt had been frowning in worry as he listened to Mike talk with the man. "Bill O'Brien doesn't...doesn't raise marijuana or anything like that, does he?"

"He doesn't even raise a garden," chortled the storekeeper.

Moments later, the girls trudged after the boys along a rutted jeep road leading out of the cottage village. "Why would Walt ask such a question?" Caylin whispered. "It was embarrassing." She hung back with Hannah, not wanting to walk with Walt just now.

"You're new around here," Hannah said. "Maybe Walt's a little too cautious. But we sure don't want to become drug runners by mistake. He was afraid that Mike's being tricked into getting a load of drugs, that's all. It's happened to people before."

"I'm sure Mike knows what he's doing," Caylin protested. "Mr. O'Brien sent him twenty dollars in advance, along with a letter promising another thirty when the job is done."

"Well, we'll see what happens. Let's catch up with the guys."

"Daddy didn't say he'd hired *girls* to carry his stuff to market." An hour of steady hiking had passed, and a ragged girl met them in a clearing in front of a log cabin. The girl was about Hannah's age. But she reminded Hannah of Mell Sampson when the Sampsons first came to Beaver Island—rough and a little intimidating.

"Hi," Hannah said, ignoring the insult. "I'm Hannah."

"And I'm Caylin—that's Walt and Mike." Caylin jerked her thumb toward the boys, who stood back in surprise at their ungracious greeter.

"Name's Rosie—Wild Rosie. Put 'er there!" Rosie reached out, insisting that first the girls, then the guys join her in a lengthy, laughing, hand-slapping greeting.

"Now I'll go get my old man." Rosie turned and hurried toward the rough log cabin. Hannah and Caylin watched in concern. Rosie limped as though her right leg was lame. Once she even cried out, doubling over in pain.

The cabin door opened. A thin, barefoot, intelligent-looking woman with wire-rim glasses stepped outside. She wore patched jeans and a ratty shirt, like her daughter. Hannah noticed, though, that the lady's hair was carefully brushed and tied back with a leather thong. "I'm Heather O'Brien," she said pleasantly. "One of you Mike Wilson?"

"I'm Mike." Mike offered his hand.

"Nice to meet you," Heather smiled. "Bill's in the cellar packing the stuff up right now. Why don't you fellows go down and help him." She pointed to an open cellar door that led beneath the cabin from outdoors.

"Sure," said Mike. "Coming, Walt?"

"Why not?" Walt hurried after Mike.

Hannah and Caylin looked at each other. Whatever the stuff was that Bill O'Brien was packing would need to be carried to the boat, two miles away. The sooner the job was done, the girls knew, the sooner they'd get started back home.

They were silently debating whether they should go help the boys when Mrs. O'Brien spoke. "Oh, you girls stay out of there. It's not much of a cellar, just a hole in the ground, really. There's not room in there for anyone else."

"Well, I guess we'll just wait and help carry the stuff to the boat then," Caylin said.

"You shouldn't even have to do that." Mrs. O'Brien nodded toward a homemade wooden wheelbarrow standing beside a stump.

Rosie reappeared and sat on the log which served as the cabin's doorstep. "Ouch!" she cried. Rosie bent over, fighting tears and holding her belly. Then she swore.

"Rosie, how you talk!" her mother corrected. "She gets that from her daddy, I guess," she apologized. "You've been complaining of a bellyache since yesterday, Rosie. Why don't you lie down, or at least take some baking soda in warm water?"

"Can't lie down," Rosie moaned. "And I tried baking soda already. It made me throw up. It doesn't hurt so much if I just move around a little." Holding her middle with both hands, Rosie scooted back inside the cabin.

Walt appeared out of the cellar just then, lugging a plastic garbage bag so full that he struggled to carry it. He plopped it into the wheelbarrow, then rested against his burden, panting. "There's lots more," he gasped.

"They pay a good price for that stuff in New York," Heather explained. "Chinese natural food stores all sell it for medicine."

"What is it?" Hannah had to know.

"Didn't Bill say in his letter? It's ginseng roots."

"Told ya." Caylin grinned at Hannah and poked her in the ribs.

Mrs. O'Brien smiled. "I understand. The Maine State Police have been here twice looking for marijuana they think we're raising. I guess you can't blame people for being suspicious, but Bill likes to live way out here like this."

Mike came out of the cellar just then, followed by Bill O'Brien. Both carried bags of ginseng root as heavy as Walt's. Hannah thought at first that Mr. O'Brien looked like Sam Sampson before Sam shaved his beard. But she quickly noticed a difference. When Mr. O'Brien talked, he sounded educated. His words were clipped and precise, almost like Lucy LaVerdiere's.

"We have three more bags still to come, Heather," Bill said. "We'll have money enough from this shipment to live in a bit of comfort, I think."

"Oh, Bill, I hope so. But you can't possibly take all that in one wheelbarrow load!"

"I've offered these guys an extra twenty each to take a second trip down to the lake with the wheelbarrow. I'll send them the money when our check comes."

"I think Rosie's worse." Mrs. O'Brien changed from happy to somber.

"Let's take her temperature again. If she's running a fever, I want to use the storekeeper's CB radio to call the county health nurse for advice."

Both parents hurried inside while Hannah and the others waited by the wheelbarrow.

The O'Briens looked worried when they returned.

"What was it?" Hannah asked, concerned.

"A hundred and one," said Heather. "Bill's going to radio the nurse as soon as he gets to The City Trading Post."

"You guys might as well stay here," Walt said, nodding at Hannah and Caylin. "Mike and I will steady the load while Mr. O'Brien pushes. Three's enough. Oh and, Han?"

"Yeah?"

"Take care of Papa's radio. I couldn't leave it in the boat." He glanced at where he had left it on a boulder, carefully wrapped in a big bandanna.

☀ ☀ ☀ ☀ ☀ ☀ ☀

The girls huddled with Mrs. O'Brien by Rosie's cot in the cabin corner. Heather held the thermometer up to the afternoon sunlight streaming through the window. "Two and a half," the mother muttered in dismay.

"That's bad," worried Caylin. "Mine went that high just before they took my appendix out."

"Appendicitis?" Mrs. O'Brien looked at Caylin in alarm.

"Mom, it hurts," Rosie groaned.

"I know, darling." Heather soaked a washcloth in cold water, wrung it out, and placed it on her daughter's forehead.

"She's getting worse fast," Caylin said quietly. Her voice was filled with fear.

"May...may we pray with you?" Hannah peered at Rosie's mom.

"Let's do." Heather O'Brien knelt beside Rosie's bed. At once she began to ask Jesus to bless and heal her daughter, finally thanking Him for His promise to supply all their needs.

Surprised at Heather's prayer, Hannah and Caylin only said "Amen" when she was finished.

"God will heal my baby," Mrs. O'Brien said firmly, standing up.

"Oh-h-h-h-h-h-h!" Rosie moaned.

"Where does it hurt the worst?" Caylin asked.

"The right side of my belly, down low."

"That's where my appendix hurt, too," Caylin murmured.

"Bill and the boys should be back." Heather glanced at a wind-up alarm clock ticking on a shelf. "It's been more'n two hours."

"How's my Wild Rosie?" Bill O'Brien tried to sound cheerful as he strode into the cabin.

"Worse," Heather reported grimly. "Did you get the nurse on the radio?"

"No." Bill swore. "Radio battery is flat. The store-keeper says it's too late in the season to spend money on a new one, for the amount of business he gets."

Hannah thought she had never heard anyone go from cheerful to gloomy so quickly. But fear and worry will do strange things to people, she knew.

"Bill, we should pray, not swear."

"Sorry." He looked at the girls sheepishly.

"We have been praying, Mr. O'Brien," Caylin said quietly. "Rosie has appendicitis, same as I had last year."

Hannah got another surprise. Silly, happy-go-lucky Caylin could also be calm and full of assurance. And she seemed to know what was wrong with Rosie.

"Suppose the girl's mistaken?" Bill O'Brien glanced at Caylin, then at Rosie, then back to his wife. Hannah figured he was arguing with himself. Whether Caylin was right or wrong, one thing seemed certain—Rosie needed a doctor, fast!

"If only we had a radio, we could call the forest service's rescue squad." Mr. O'Brien turned to Walt, suddenly remembering. "Didn't you bring your boat radio?"

"It won't work," Walt squeaked weakly. "The battery's in the boat."

"Well-ll." Bill sighed, glancing at the wall where an old-fashioned wooden telephone hung. "We haven't got that thing wired up yet, but it puts out twelve volts when you turn the crank, just the same as your boat's battery. *Go get your radio!*"

"Yes, sir!" Walt ran for the door. Rosie's father had thundered those last words.

Mr. O'Brien ripped the old phone off the wall without bothering to remove the screws. He grabbed a spool of wire from a drawer and began to connect lengths of it to the phone.

"Bill's got an engineering degree in electronics," Heather said quietly. "He can make an antique telephone run a modern radio if anyone can."

Ten minutes later, the Maine Forest Service rescue helicopter and medical emergency team were on their way.

※ ※ ※ ※ ※ ※ ※

"What do you suppose this ginseng is worth, Walt?" Hannah helped her brother and Caylin lift the last bag into the boat. Mike had walked back to the Trading Post to leave Mr. O'Brien's wheelbarrow for him to get later.

"Bill said it would bring in several thousand dollars. He told Mike and me that he has a deal with the railway freight office in Laketon. The station master will crate this for him and ship it to a warehouse in New York for a share of the profit." Walt shook his head. "What a way to live!"

"You and Hannah live pretty far out in the boonies, yourselves," laughed Caylin.

The loud "lop-lop-lop-lop-lop-lop-lop" of the forest service helicopter's blade drowned out their voices just then. Hannah, Walt, and Caylin waved at the passing helicopter as Mike returned to the boat. They watched for a moment as the aircraft carrying Rosie shot off toward Foxcroft Regional Hospital and finally vanished from view across Moosehead Lake.

"Did you give them a tract packet, Mike?" Caylin asked, as soon as Mike started the boat and headed down Spencer Bay.

"Sure did. I left it on their kitchen table—with a twenty dollar bill inside. Mr. O'Brien says it will be six weeks, at least, until he gets paid for this shipment."

Hannah and Walt stared at each other in surprise for a moment.

"I guess they need the money more than you do right now," Walt said finally.

Nodding in agreement, Hannah settled happily back into her swivel seat. She hoped they hadn't seen the last of the O'Briens.

Chapter Nineteen

A Surprise
Package

"What is *this?*" exclaimed Hannah one afternoon. The big motorboat that pulled up to the dock in front of Beaver Lodge was painted metallic brown, and the smiling delivery man who stepped out wore a brown uniform. Hannah had seen a United Parcel Service truck in Laketon several times, and Mama sometimes ordered packages which UPS delivered at Aunt Theresa's house.

But a UPS boat?

"Package for a Miss Hannah Parmenter," announced the delivery man. "Sign here, please."

Hannah signed and took the box, which was about twice the size of a shoe box and marked 'fragile.' How long has UPS had a delivery boat?" she asked, surprised.

"First day, ma'am. And you're my first stop!"

"No kidding?!"

The delivery man chuckled. "We're trying this as an experiment. There are several cottage villages on this lake out of reach of our trucks. So we're offering boat service until Labor Day. See y'." He hopped into the boat and roared off down the lake.

"It's about time we had some services, like on the mainland," said Mama, who had always lived in the city until the family moved to Beaver Island. She was waiting on the porch when Hannah came up the path with the package. "Now if Bangor Hydroelectric would only get us a line out here, we wouldn't be dependent on that diesel generator your father is forever tinkering on."

"We weren't dependent on the generator when we first moved to the island, Mama," Hannah said, grinning slyly.

"Kerosene lamps and an old-fashioned icebox," Mama groaned, remembering.

"Maybe the Maine State Highway Department will build us a bridge. We're *only* three miles off shore from Laketon." Papa was teasing, of course. Hannah knew by the tone of his voice that he preferred to have Beaver Island left alone. Mama wanted city conveniences. Papa wanted the woods, the lake, the solitude.

Mama hugged Papa. "I know, Harry," she sighed. "But you do get a lot of backwoods living each fall when you take those hunting parties into the Allagash Wilderness and live in primitive camps."

"Doesn't anyone wish to know what's in my package?" Hannah held her box up.

"Sure, honey," Mama murmured, pointing to a small table on the porch.

"This'll help." Papa pulled out his pocket knife and unfolded the blade so Hannah could cut the tape. "Why, it's from the university!" he exclaimed, noticing the return address.

"That was certainly nice of Professor Frankenmuth to send you an Indian vase," Mama said moments later.

"Well, the college students gave me a pretty good tip," laughed Hannah, remembering the fifty dollars she had put in her dresser drawer. "This is just frosting on the cake."

"I'm not so sure." Papa wore a puzzled frown as he stared at the vase, shiny and new-looking in the sunlight. "Didn't the professor send a letter?"

"Nothing, Papa." Hannah showed him the box, empty except for the plastic bubble-wrap that had protected the vase.

"Check inside."

Hannah reached within. "Here it is!" She drew out a folded typewritten letter. As she did, a small envelope slipped out onto the table, and a news clipping fluttered to the floor. Papa picked up the clipping.

"Archaeologist Refutes Vase's Antiquity," read the headline.

"What does it mean?" asked Hannah.

"It means," said Papa, "that this is not an old vase."

"I can see that," Hannah protested. "It's shiny and new!"

"Precisely," Papa agreed. He read the news clipping, then passed it to Hannah, who passed Papa the letter she'd just read.

"Will someone please tell me what's going on!" insisted Mama, who was holding the small envelope. "This seems to be a card addressed to Melanie Sampson. But *what* is in your letter, Hannah?"

"Remember that old, dirty vase with bones in it that Hunter and Mell found? This is it."

"It can't be." Mama was astonished.

"How do we know Professor Frankenmuth didn't just buy a new one from Ben Bear-of-the-Woods on Abnaki Island and keep the real one?" Papa, too, was not convinced.

"'Cause Mell scratched her initials on it. See!" Hannah turned the vase over in triumph. Sure enough, there in the glazing were Mell's initials, *MS.* They appeared only when Hannah tipped the vase toward the sun.

"Well, I'll be a monkey's uncle!" said Papa.

"Like the professor says," Hannah concluded, "this vase was made by Ben Bear-of-the-Woods. It was left on our island by an intruder, who tossed it on the woodchuck's dirt pile."

"So how did those old Indian bones get inside the vase?" asked Mama.

"Simple," Hannah chuckled. "Not just the vase, but the whole pile of dirt dug up by the woodchuck was full of old bones."

"I guess a few bones might land in the vase when the chuck was digging," Mama agreed.

"And if it hadn't been for that careless camper, the old Indian cemetery would probably never have been found," Hannah said, hugging Papa. "Y'know," she added, "what I thought was going to be just another adventure to unravel the mystery of the old Indian cemetery sure led to a lot more!"

"Such as?" Papa's eyes twinkled, but his face was serious.

"Such as new friends, like the professor and Lucy and Chief Littledeer! You and Mama can't *imagine* what I've learned about people. But I've got to take the vase and the notes from the professor over to Mell Sampson, 'cause the vase is really hers." She raced down the porch steps and ran off toward the path that led through the woods to the old Sampson place beyond Bald Hill.

"And *I've* got to find a way to keep this island more private for our hotel guests," Papa told Mama, rubbing his chin. "United Parcel Service with a boat! Next thing will be Macy's Thanksgiving Day Parade wanting to march through here!"

"Aren't you being just a little extreme, Harry?" Mama laughed, kissing Papa's cheek.

"A little," he admitted, chuckling. "Oh, but look here! We have a visitor."

"Chief Littledeer!" Mama cried. She and Papa hurried down the steps as the chief stepped from a rented boat he had just tied to the dock. They met the shaman as he strode up the walk, dressed in his ceremonial deerskins.

※ ※ ※ ※ ※ ※ ※

"Oh!" Hannah clapped her hand over her mouth, startled. "Mr. Littledeer!" she squealed. Hannah had returned by the back way and slipped through the kitchen, expecting to find Papa chatting with a hotel guest. Instead, she found the chief, with his ceremonial headdress laid across his knees. On the coffee table lay the small leather case in which Chief Littledeer carried his calumet pipe. "You've come to...?"

"Yes, to do a final dedication of the cemetery. I got your brother's note, and I'm glad he is so honest," he said, nodding toward Walt, who sat on the edge of the fireplace.

"Because of the beads and the bones?" Hannah was embarrassed that Mr. Littledeer had to return all the way from Canada because of Walt's carelessness. But she was also proud that her brother had written to Chief Littledeer like he said he would.

"That, too. He's told me all about it." Chief Littledeer smiled at Walt again. "I had to pay a visit to my old friend, Professor Frankenmuth, at the university," he explained. "He and I—we often work together to discover the past of my ancient people. So it was only a short ride over here this morning from Bangor. And I'd also love to have several of those beautiful puppies, if dear Mell and little Paul haven't given them all away." He chuckled. "You see, I had much to come to Beaver Island for."

"They still have five pups," Hannah said, practically beaming. "And they're darling."

"I can't imagine a better mix of breeds for a child's pet," the chief agreed. "I need them as special gifts for my granddaughters."

"Do...do you need a ride across the island to the burial site, Chief?" Walt volunteered.

"Oh, no." He motioned toward the dock. "I'll just buzz around with the boat."

Two hours later, right after the guests had been fed, Hannah and Walt were about to eat in the kitchen with Papa and Mama. Just then, Mr. Littledeer returned. Mama quickly set a place for him at the family table.

"How did the ceremony go?" Papa asked.

Hannah had fixed toasted corned beef sandwiches on rye bread for lunch, and Mr. Littledeer was just taking a bite. He chewed for several moments, taking his time, thinking.

"All right," he answered slowly, after a while. Unlike the chief's last visit to Beaver Lodge, he did not seem to wish to discuss his religious ceremony with the family.

"I'm glad you can use the puppies," Hannah murmured, changing the subject. "Your granddaughters will be thrilled." She then excused herself to use the phone.

"I'm sure they'll be pleased." The chief smiled, glancing at the clock. "I've got a bus to catch in

Laketon," he said. "Doctor Frankenmuth is expecting me. He and Ben Bear-of-the-Woods are meeting the bus in Bangor."

"Ben?" Papa was surprised.

"He and his mother are from our tribe of Micmacs, on the Miramichi River in New Brunswick. Ben and his mother are Christians, like the professor," he added curiously.

Hannah put down the phone. "Will you be helping the professor?" She was not sure just how to word her question. "Helping him dig up...?"

"Another cemetery?" the chief finished for her. "No, child. I still want very much to learn more about my ancestors, but there will be no more ceremonies, no more death for me. Hans Frankenmuth, Ben Bear, and I—we have been talking for many weeks about *life*. Jesus said, 'I am the resurrection and the life,'" he quoted. "I expect to find that life with Jesus this afternoon. Harry and Sandy, Hannah and Walt, I thank you. You Parmenters have meant more to me by your kindness than you can imagine." LeRoi Littledeer rose and walked toward the porch, just as Melanie and Paul scurried up the steps with a box of squirming puppies.

That evening in her secret cave deep under the hay, Hannah was writing in her diary. The sun had set, and she had propped Papa's rechargeable flashlight up so it shined across the hay bale that served as her desk. Hannah felt secure and safe, for she had carefully hidden the mouth of the tunnel to her cave with a bale of hay when she crawled in. And tonight there were no boys outside to pester her with green apples!

Dear diary,

Hannah penned,

Life is so full of surprises. Today God used the delivery of a vase, once tossed away by a tourist, to show me that even Papa and Mama don't have all the answers to life's problems, even though I used to think they did. Papa loves solitude. Mama loves crowds. I guess they decided to compromise by moving to a lake island, then inviting the crowd to come find us.

Hannah put her pen down, thinking. Then she wrote some more:

*Chief Littledeer came back today with the biggest surprise of all. He wants to become a Christian! And though I was **BURSTING** to ask him to trust Jesus right then, I didn't. I know that, in His time, God will finish what He started in Chief Littledeer's life."*

Chapter Twenty

Two Islands and Two Views

"Mama, I've *got* to get over to Foxcroft to see Rosie before she goes home," Hannah insisted the morning after Chief Littledeer's visit. "If we wait until she goes back north of Spencer Bay, I may never see her again." Hannah was clearing the breakfast dishes away after the last guests had eaten.

Hannah had prayed for Rosie O'Brien every day since her trip up Spencer Bay with Mike, Walt, and Caylin. Heather O'Brien had sent a note explaining that Rosie's appendix had burst before the doctors could operate. Rosie would spend the rest of August and possibly part of September in the hospital in Foxcroft because of this.

"Maybe you're old enough to travel by yourself," Mama said thoughtfully. "Why don't you call the depot right now and see if there's a bus to Foxcroft and back today? If there is, call the hospital and see if this is a good day to visit."

"Super!" Hannah dropped her dishes in the suds-filled sink and grabbed for the phone with her still-wet hands. "Oh, Mama," she said, thinking of something, "can I ask Caylin to come along? Seeing Rosie would be just as important to her."

"Go ahead," Mama chuckled. "It'll be safer for you two to travel together, and I'll bet Rosie will be twice as happy."

"We don't have a Rosie O'Brien here." The hospital receptionist peered at Hannah and Caylin. "Are you sure she's registered under that name?"

Hannah frowned. She had talked to Mrs. O'Brien this morning. Rosie *had* to be here.

"Wild Rosie, maybe?" Caylin suggested. "That's what she called herself."

"Oh!" The receptionist smiled mysteriously. "That Miss O'Brien. She's in Room 236. Her mother's there right now."

Hannah stared in surprise at the name on the door of Room 236: *Wylda R. O'Brien.* Then she giggled. "Rosie lives up to her name, I guess," she told Caylin softly, knocking on the door.

Mrs. O'Brien opened the door wide and ushered them in. "I kept your visit a secret," she whispered, her eyes sparkling.

Rosie beamed when she saw who it was. "Hi, Caylin. Hi, Hannah," she chirped. "Can you believe I get to go home tomorrow?"

"Our Wylda Rose is almost ready for a wild life in the wilderness again," Heather O'Brien confirmed.

"Not so wild from now on, Mom." Rosie looked at Hannah almost shyly. "Jesus answered your prayer."

"What...what prayer?" Hannah was startled. Rosie could not possibly have known that Hannah was praying daily for Rosie's salvation, as well as for her healing.

"You prayed beside my bed in our cabin before the helicopter came, remember?"

"I do remember." There had been some very confusing moments right after Walt used Papa's radio to call the forest service rescue. Hannah did remember praying, but what she'd said, she'd forgotten completely. "Why don't you tell me about it," Hannah suggested.

"You prayed that Jesus would look into my wild heart and give me faith to trust Him." Rosie smiled and continued. "Then you asked Jesus to remind me that He died on the cross for my sins. I knew that already, of course, because Mom had explained it to me many times. But somehow Jesus' dying for me became real when I heard someone my own age praying for me like she really cared, and like Jesus was a friend right there listening."

Hannah and Caylin were so excited by Rosie's news that they both started talking at once. When the visit was over, Hannah had Rosie's promise to visit her on Beaver Island someday. Hannah knew Rosie might not be able to come soon, but a *someday* promise was still a promise, she thought happily.

※ ※ ※ ※ ※ ※ ※

"It's for you, honey." Mama handed Hannah the phone.

"I'm calling from the Greyhound depot in Laketon," said the voice with the clipped Canadian accent on the phone. "How have you been?"

'Bean?' No, 'been,' Lucy had said. "I've bean just fine. How've you bean?" Hannah teased. "Yes," she squealed, even before Lucy could ask, "I can come get you in one of Papa's boats." It was right after Labor Day, and most of the hotel guests at

Beaver Lodge had returned to the big cities. There would be few guests until the fall leaf color season, so a boat to go after a friend in Laketon was no problem.

"Super!" Lucy LaVerdiere said. "I'll meet you at the dock."

"Shouldn't I have Uncle Joe pick you up with the car? It's a long walk with a suitcase."

"Oh," laughed Lucy, "I've already checked my bags in at the university dorm. All I'm carrying is my backpack."

"This is a beautiful island, Hannah. You must love it here."

"Is there any other place to be?" Hannah teased.

"There's Prince Edward Island," Lucy laughed.

The girls were silent for some moments. It was a cool late summer evening on the edge of the northern wilderness, and the high barn window that looked out over the hillside pasture and hayfields had been closed. As usual with barn windows, it was dirty with fly specks. But since a hard frost a few days earlier had sent the flies and mosquitoes into hibernation, the girls were not bothered. Hannah reached over and grabbed the window. She pushed it open, then pinned the sash up with the old spike Papa had left hanging on a string for this purpose. She was glad Mama had given her and Lucy permission to camp out in the barn tonight.

"Beautiful!" Lucy murmured again, her view now clear. She and Hannah gazed up the pasture hill, where the moonlight made every stone, every fence post, every cedar rail glitter with a silvery sheen.

"What's that?!" Lucy cried. She pointed to a feathered creature as big as Smokey, Papa's big Plymouth Rock barnyard rooster. This airborne beast's bulky body sailed on massive wings, almost as wide as Papa's arms outstretched. The big bird's ghostly shadow glided eerily ahead of it as it sailed across the moonlit field.

Suddenly the creature folded its great wings and dropped like a lead sinker. It beat the air furiously, then rose, a hapless hare hanging from its cruel, sharp talons, struggling in vain to get free.

"What is it?" Lucy cried again.

A fearful memory of one of Sam Sampson's fancy Vietnamese pigs about to become supper for this same dangerous feathered dive bomber flitted through Hannah's mind. "The great horned owl," she gasped, recognizing her old enemy. "There's one hare that's wishing right now it had been caught in one of your wire snares instead."

Both girls held their breath as the owl soared into the branches of a tall hemlock beyond the old stone wall to eat his supper.

Hannah turned to Lucy. "Say, you said you grew up in the city. How do you know about catching rabbits?"

"Charlottetown, P.E.I., is hardly Toronto or New York," chuckled Lucy. "We kept a garden, like many folks there. One of our neighbors had a hutch full of rabbits, and they got loose."

"And they multiplied, of course. Rabbits are very good at math," Hannah laughed.

"Did they ever! They were eating up the gardens for blocks in every direction. So an elderly neighbor who grew up in the woods in New Brunswick showed us how to make wire rabbit snares."

"Why do you want to become an archaeologist,

Lucy?" Hannah's mind ran back to the weeks of early summer. She had watched with great interest as Lucy and the other college students dug into the old burial ground. Shards of pottery, beads, hatchets of both stone and steel, bones that were hundreds or even thousands of years old—these came out of the gravel ridge.

Hannah remembered her surprise when Professor Frankenmuth showed her human teeth that were nearly worn out. She had seen teeth with cavities, and Hannah knew that cows sometimes wore out their teeth. When Papa bought Molly to give them fresh milk on Beaver Island, he had guessed her age by her teeth.

But humans?

"Yes," the professor had said gravely, "these people were grain eaters."

"Grain eaters?" Hannah had been puzzled.

"These Abnakis were farmers," said the professor. "They raised corn."

"How can you tell from their teeth?"

"They're badly worn from eating corn ground with stone tools. Bits of stone got mixed with the flour, and this wore their teeth out."

Now, weeks later, it was September, and that night in the barn Hannah turned to Lucy. "I guess you can learn a lot of interesting stuff about how people lived long ago," said Hannah.

"A lot of it helps us understand how people think today," Lucy said thoughtfully. "But I'm not sure I want to be an archaeologist."

"You're not?" Hannah was surprised. "But you're studying in college to become one."

"The more I learn about my ancestors, the Micmac branch of the Abnakis, the more I realize that God has something different for me."

"What...what do you mean?"

"Many of these people worship nature, like the Native North Americans of long, long ago," said Lucy.

"They worship creation instead of the Creator." Hannah remembered reading a warning about that in her Bible.

"This summer," said Lucy, "I met Chief Little-deer, who used to worship nature and pray to the angry spirits. I saw how the love of Christian friends such as Ben Bear, Professor Frankenmuth, and your family reached him with Christ's love." Lucy smiled, thinking. "I love my Abnaki Indian nation— the Micmacs in Canada, the Penobscots, here in Maine. Now that I've seen what love can do through ordinary people, I want to be a part of sharing Jesus with those of my people who don't know Him."

"But you said what love can do through *ordinary* people. The professor isn't exactly ordinary."

"Doctor Frankenmuth and I talked about that," Lucy answered softly. "And you know what?"

"What?" Hannah leaned closer, waiting.

"It was your brother, Walt, who finally made Chief Littledeer stop doubting. He has all the rough edges of a typical teen boy," she chuckled. "But when Mr. Littledeer got Walt's note apologizing for taking those bones and beads, the chief saw a side of Christian life he'd never seen before."

"What do you mean?" Hannah was puzzled.

"Walt's action in taking that stuff back to the grave, even though he didn't really steal it—this told the chief that Walt could love his neighbor as he loves himself, like Jesus said to do."

"Love opens a door in the heart for sure," Hannah agreed, thinking of Rosie O'Brien, who wasn't really as rough as she pretended to be.

"And there are so many hearts that need to be opened by love," Lucy said. "Just think, *all the world* needs to be given the Gospel of Christ."

"Lucy," said Hannah, "life for you must seem like a winding road in the woods. You never can know what's around the next bend. You're a college archaeology student for a while. Then just a few weeks later you've decided to become a missionary."

"God knows what's around all our bends," Lucy said softly. "But it helps to recognize the changes in our lives when they begin to happen. For me, I need to wait now to find out *how* God wants to use me to share the Gospel. It could be that archaeology will play a part in that. Do I guess that you're about to round a bend, too?"

"Yup," agreed Hannah, a mysterious tone to her voice.

"Oh?" Lucy raised an eyebrow.

"Boys."

"I am sure there's a lot more around *that* bend than just boys," Lucy chuckled. "Guys can seem awfully important, though."

"Oh?" It was Hannah's turn to raise an eyebrow.

"I've been around that bend myself," Lucy said knowingly. "I'm not even sure I'm all the way around it yet."

Sleepy now, Hannah rolled over in her sleeping bag and stared far up into the rafters of the old barn where a barn swallow had built her nest. Earlier that summer Walt had helped Hannah put a ladder up there to check on newborn birds. They were helpless little creatures without feathers, completely dependent on Mama Swallow to feed and warm them. Weeks later, Hannah had watched in glee as Mama Swallow pushed her fledglings, one by one, from their secure mud-and-straw nest to try a maiden voyage far above the barn's open central floor.

Now, as Hannah peered up into the shadows, she could count five nearly grown swallows crowded onto the edge of the nest. In only weeks, she knew, these birds would wing southward with Mama Swallow, borne on wings grown strong from weeks of practice flights.

It occurred to Hannah that two birds of an entirely different feather than swallows perched in their sleeping bags in the haymow just now. One, like the swallows above them, had already left her nest on Prince Edward Island, taking longer and longer flights until at last this bird could fly alone, with God as her guide.

But the fledgling bird of Beaver Island? Hannah unconsciously slipped deeper into her down-filled bag, enjoying the warmth of her nest against the night's chill. A cloud passed over the moon, and the swallows on the edge of their nest vanished into the gloom of night. Hannah closed her eyes, asking Jesus to see her safely through the night and bear her around the unseen bends in her road.

Hannah slept in untroubled happiness until red dawn streaked the beams above her with light. In the tie-up below, she heard Walt calling Molly from her nighttime pasture for the cow's morning milking. Above, on the barn's rafters, the twittering of dozens of swallows caught Hannah's ear. Unzipping her sleeping bag, Hannah hunkered with her knees under her chin and began to lace up her sneakers to face a brand new day.